GW00372164

Stranger Things Have Happened

Carmelita McGrath

Also by Carmelita McGrath

FICTION

Walking to Shenak—1994

POETRY

Poems on Land and on Water—1992
To The New World—1997

Stranger Things Have Happened

Carmelita McGrath

killick press
an imprint of Creative Publishers

St. John's, Newfoundland
1999

© 1999, Carmelita McGrath

THE CANADA COUNCIL | LE CONSEIL DES ARTS
FOR THE ARTS | DU CANADA
SINCE 1957 | DEPUIS 1957

We acknowledge the support of The Canada Council for the Arts
for our publishing program.

We acknowledge the financial support of the
Department for Canadian Heritage
for our publishing program.

All rights reserved. No part of this work covered by the copyrights hereon may
be reproduced or used in any form or by any means — graphic, electronic or
mechanical — without the prior written permission of the publisher. Any
requests for photocopying, recording, taping or information storage and
retrieval systems of any part of this book shall be directed in writing to the
Canadian Reprography Collective, One Yonge Street, Suite 1900,
Toronto, Ontario M5E 1E5.

∞ Printed on acid-free paper

Published by
KILLICK PRESS
an imprint of CREATIVE BOOK PUBLISHING
a division of 10366 Newfoundland Limited
a Robinson-Blackmore Printing & Publishing associated company
P.O. Box 8660, St. John's, Newfoundland A1B 3T7

FIRST EDITION
Typeset in 12 point Garamond

Printed in Canada by:
ROBINSON-BLACKMORE PRINTING & PUBLISHING

Canadian Cataloguing in Publication Data

McGrath, Carmelita
    Stranger things have happened

    ISBN 1-894294-10-6

I. Title

PS8575.G68S8   1999   C813'.54   C99-950175-7
PR9199.3.M42425S8   1999

For Jerry, Don, Josephine and Tina
and, as always, for Leah

Contents

Stranger Things Have Happened

*T*he evening I saw the angel I was looking for my parents. I'd
dawdled my way home from school after playing alone for
awhile by the river, where I was not supposed to go by myself.
Watching the black water rush under the first thin skin of winter,
I had thrown rocks to hear the ice tinkle and shatter like glass.
All the way home, the sticky, early snow sucked at my feet like
an extra force of gravity pulling me to earth. My shoes were
soaked. It wasn't late enough yet in the year to be wearing boots.
I remember it was early November, just after All Souls, and
darkening early, the sky the colour purple cloth fades to when
you leave it too long in the sun.

I was thinking about whether it was bread day and, if it was,
what my mother might have made for me to eat. Sometimes on
bread day, she'd take some leftover dough, divide it in pieces,
stretch the pieces out flat and thin, and lay them on brown
paper. Then she'd spread a little butter along their lengths,
sprinkle them with a mixture of cinnamon and sugar, roll them
and bake them so that I could tear their hot sweetness between
my teeth when I got home. I always closed my eyes when I ate
cinnamon rolls, because cinnamon would take me somewhere I
had never been, only imagined, and the soft breath of that island
would stir against my face, thawing it out, banishing the frost.

I opened the door, sniffing for cinnamon. But there was
nothing only stillness and silence and the stale smell my father's

cigarettes left behind. And then I remembered Mr. Thomas. They'd be at Mr. Thomas's wake.

It was only across the road, and a short ways down the lane, Mr. Thomas's house. I dropped my bookbag in our porch and set off in my wet shoes.

The angel appeared in the form of a small light, a tiny, yellow flame. I knew what it was right away. About two feet ahead of me, just higher than my head, it seemed to propel itself by flickering. I turned into the path to Mr. Thomas's house, and the angel turned with me. I smiled at it, and folded my hands and bowed. The light from the windows gave out onto the snow-covered yard, a flood of yellow with the edges darkly purple. I knew if the angel was just a reflection it would disappear in this greater light. But it didn't. It held its course right to the door, then dimmed. Disappeared. *Gone in, for Mr. Thomas's soul.*

In the kitchen the adults were so thick they pressed up against cupboards, the sink, the stove. Someone patted my hair as if any child would do. I could smell rum and fruitcake; pea soup rumbled like an engine on the stove. I turned my body left and right, flattening it so I could pass like a fish among undersea rocks. Swimming this way, I came to the arch that opened into the hall, and crossed over. Through the front room doorway, I could see my mother on one of the hard kitchen chairs that were placed in a row, eight of them making a line away from the coffin.

"Jesus," Mr. David said behind me, making me jump out of my skin, "it looks like clinic day at the hospital. I don't know what Thomas thinks he's doing here, though, there's no hope for him."

And all the women made black looks at Mr. David, who had a big drink in his hand. But he was right, and the clinic had looked just this way the one time I was there, when the cut the rusty nail had made in my foot had grown dark red and ragged around the edges. Just like the clinic except for the coffin, shiny and dark, with brass on it like you'd find on the drawers of a nice sideboard.

Because I had just seen an angel, I said a silent prayer for Mr. David, *Please, God, don't be too hard on Mr. David, he's only on the drink and sad over his brother dying.* And just for a second I saw in my mind's eye Mr. Thomas and Mr. David as little boys down by the wharf watching the boats come in, waiting with their pans and knives ready to cut out cod tongues. For sure the angel was showing me this picture, because I had never seen such a clear thing in my mind's eye before.

"Come over, Lily," my mother said, crooking her finger. "Didn't have trouble finding me, did you?"

"No," I said, not wanting to hurt her feelings with the cold house and the want of cinnamon buns.

She made a spot for me on the chair, and pressed her hands over my damp mittens. "Take off your wet stuff," she said, "you'll catch your death of cold." So I did, and pressed against her although she was always telling me lately I was too old for this.

"Your daddy'll be here when he gets out of the woods. Go up and say a prayer for *him*, now, out of respect."

"After," I said.

Leaning up against her, I stole glances at Mr. Thomas, and after a while I got used to him enough to stare. He had on a black suit, and a white shirt and black tie. His grey hair was combed and wetted down so it wouldn't stick up like a cock of hay the way it usually did. His hands were in a strange place where you wouldn't put your hands, folded high on his chest with his prayer book under them and his brown glass rosary beads woven around his fingers like he was pulling on them, trying to haul himself up. His face was the quietest face I'd ever seen, with not a stir in it, although if you looked long enough you could see his eyelids twitch a little and his lips pucker as his held breath escaped.

People came up to the coffin, and crossed themselves and prayed, and most of them finished by laying a hand on Mr. Thomas's forehead. Some of the children even did this, whispering "touch him," "no, you touch him," but you wouldn't catch me doing it. They say if you touch a dead person, you will never dream of him, and he won't be able to come back to you in your sleep, and talk away to you like he was living, only cold and white and tattered in places, and full of stories of the land of the dead. I watched and listened.

"My God, he looks so young and healthy," I heard a woman say, but then a great snowstorm started, and the wind carried the drift into my eyes and carried me away somewhere.

When I woke, my father was in the room, and my mother was offering me bread with butter and molasses. I stuffed it in my mouth, suddenly cold and starving.

"We'll go now," my mother said.

"I don't want to go yet."

She gave me a queer look. "Poor tired little thing," she said.

"Can't I stay with Dad?"

"No."

I could see that all the women and girls and young boys were leaving. It was only the men staying to sit up with the corpse. They'd be there for the night; Mr. Thomas couldn't be left alone until he was in his grave.

I caught my father's eye and he winked at me. Smiled. But behind the smile was a serious look he'd keep all night and all tomorrow. The men were taking over the row of chairs, and there were bottles and glasses of rum and beer on the floor around them. Like my father, they all looked furrowed and serious, yet all around the room there was the feeling of a holiday. "To Thomas, may angels sing him to his rest," I heard my father say as my mother tied my scarf around my droopy neck and half-carried me out into the night, and home.

Holy. It was what I carried home with me. A word that blooms in the heat.

"You're awful hot," my mother said, tucking me in. Her rough hands sanded my forehead, wore the day away. I was hot. I thought of a great fever coming to vanquish me, and before I slept a strange thought came and settled in a quiet little part of my head that I hadn't used before. *Maybe the angel had not come for Mr. Thomas, but for me.*

"Straight lines, two-by-two. No fooling around. Walk with dignity," Miss Katherine said. She moved down the line, inspecting our manners, the small tinkly school bell in her hand ready to sound an alarm. I squished my toes in the mud, enjoying the slurping sound. Miss Katherine's high heels dug deeper, leaving tracks like those of horseshoes. A blinding sun had taken the snow back to heaven.

"Now children, forward please."

We moved as one. We had all learned a slow, shuffling walk for funeral processions. It was Miss Katherine's particular pride. Give me your ragged, your snot-nosed, your undernourished, your mewling and sprawling children, and I will turn them into marchers ready to honour the dead. We snaked our way down the road, the line wavering a little but still solid, and we were joined by people coming out of their yards, all in their best clothes and hats. A plane droned overhead and we all looked up, excited, because a plane hardly ever flew over St. Patrick's, but we couldn't say "oooh" or wave to the pilot.

Miss Katherine raised her left hand, and we all stopped so fast and sudden we ran into each other. We shuffled at the top of the lane to Mr. Thomas's house, watching his horse and cart carry his coffin toward us. Then Mrs. Mary Thomas, and the grown sons and daughters, and the grandchildren, a chain from big to small.

I watched the horse, Barnaby, who often stood in summer just inside his fence and neighed at our horse. Barnaby was always tossing his head and making strange faces, wild smiles with all his teeth showing. Now he was still and slow, as if he'd been in training with Miss Katherine too.

We moved on. To the church, now. The requiem mass so lovely it made you cry even if you weren't sad. With the candles and the incense, the dark brocaded cloths, the quiet here quieter than anywhere else, the choir straining around *Eternal rest grant unto him, O Lord, and let per-pet-ual light shi-ine upon him.* Miss Katherine in the choir loft now, coaxing dignity out of the wheezy organ. Then the procession out, behind the horse again, stepping around its steaming moss-coloured droppings, up the steep hill to the graveyard, and through the rites of burial, the hard dropped clod of earth, until Miss Katherine walked by us, whispering, "Okay, children, you are dismissed. Go home to lunch."

Until that moment, I had kept my eyes in one place. The place shifted as I walked, was the stiff yellow of the dead meadows, the dark panelling of the church, the green of spruce, the grey of piled stones edging the fields. Yet it was always the one place, a point about two feet in front of my eyes. I kept looking there, as if the air itself would inflame into a small golden light and fill me with that word *holy*. But though I looked and looked, that day and after, and got regular fevers, and did all my homework and scrubbed the stairs with a brush on Saturdays, and never called Miss Katherine Rickety-Sticks behind her back, though I prayed and wished myself into being a good and quiet girl, the angel never returned.

"And then I felt him—it was a him, yes, definitely a male figure—he lifted me, right out of the waves. I just lay on the beach. I was all alone. I felt really, really warm. And then I knew I would be all right, I would heal."

The room lies stilled under her story like a meadow on the hottest day of summer. Eight of us, strangers, in this circle of chairs, enervated, sapped, wordless. Cara Thistle, failed suicide, her wrists tattooed with scars she can't stop scratching, lifted from drowning in the frigid North Atlantic. Laid gently down and warmed by a male angel with the musculature of a body-builder. God's lifeguard. Saved, after all.

Sarah Mellon, the facilitator, waits a while before asking, "Is there anyone else who wishes to speak tonight?"

Silence.

"Lily?"

"I think—not tonight, Sarah. Perhaps next time."

"As long as you know we all listen to and respect each other's experiences."

I feel my face redden, visible heat spreading down my neck. Lily the Doubter. For all her tenderness and talk of trust, Sarah has a lot of old Miss Rickety-Sticks in her. A certain brittleness that cannot be softened if it is truly part of who you are, a certain ability to embarrass without meaning it.

"I do, Sarah. And I feel—inspired. I will be ready some night." I smile at them all, make them look me in the eye. All of them have laid it on the line. Have told their stories; past fear and disbelief they have been bold in giving up their secrets. There is only me left in a locked silence. Well, me and Abram Moffat, and it is dubious whether Abe will ever tell a story in this circle. When he begins, he erupts into a blaze of languages. Moffat the prophet, he speaks in tongues.

I am here because I saw the sign in the window of Rod's Groc. & Conf. on one of those nowhere nights just before Christmas.

Stranger Things Have Happened
∞ encounters with angels in everyday life ∞
for more information call
Sarah Mellon, Facilitator, 777-5683

I am here because my father died in the oilfields of Alberta, where he had gone to work at the age of sixty, before the fishery sounded its death knell, but when its tolling could be heard faintly on the air by anyone who had an ear for it. A pipe hit him on the back of the head. Instant, they said. I am here because my baby brother, not even thought of when the angel visited me that November evening so long ago, dreamed of flying and plummeted to earth in that vast wilderness that is the interior of the island of Newfoundland. Through these vicious rents in the fabric of life, I have waited for a sign, a light, for the angel to come again, but I have been left merely bereft. I am here because I go on and on, it seems, in spite of everything, from one success to another. But I am here especially because of what happened last summer.

It happened like this. I was on the Trans-Canada, travelling home to St. John's from a weekend business seminar in Terra Nova National Park. Charged with the energy of the green hills, the sea air, the ideas floating like bright bubbles day and night, I set the cruise control and floated like a bubble myself. There was some particularly tinkly piano music on the radio, eddying and rippling like water in a small, chilly steady. The full moon, just up, silvered the highway, the indigo sky.

I woke up airborne. Once you have this sensation, you can never forget it. One minute you are travelling along, the road under you, the next minute you are in the air and heading for the ditch, and nothing can stop you. Everything slows down. There is time to pray or remonstrate. There is time to figure out what might have happened. There is time to calculate the square root of the number of miles left to carry you home. But there is no time to change anything. You might as well take your hands off the wheel now, but you don't. You hold tighter, pulling upward, as if the wheel will release the ripcord of a parachute that will, miraculously, lift you upward. Then the grate of rocks, the scrape of branches. The moon at your feet. A boxer's glove gets you right in the face. Then nothing.

I came back from nothing to a small, wavering light. "Hello? Hello!" The man behind the flashlight clearly frantic.

Narcolepsy. From one doctor's room to another I have gone, and this is the best they can tell me. Before, I would think *I was just worn out, I really must get more sleep*. Before the accident. Before I lay on a stretcher on the green verge of the ditch and saw the demented sculpture my car had become. Before I lay beneath the probes of flashlights and listened to my own loud breath and the quieter voices overlapping each other: "It's a miracle she got out of it as good as she did." "Jesus, I thought she was a goner." When my mother found out, she shook like a leaf and then got mad at me. "How could you!" she said. "In perfect driving conditions!" With her eyes, she held my hands, the closest she could come to comforting a grown woman, a reckless woman. She was letting me know she couldn't bear another loss.

She doesn't know that I can go to sleep anytime. Anywhere.

Once I almost told my mother about the angel I had seen on the evening of Mr. Thomas's wake. It was not long after my father's death. But all the words I could find sounded idiotic, as if I were stretching for some false piece of supernatural comfort. And before I could say anything, my mother had started to tell me of her plans.

"I'm leaving here, Lily. There's nothing here for me." She stroked the pale, primrose curtains, picked up a basket of dried wildflowers she'd arranged and set it down. "I was going to leave, anyway." She had it all planned. So quickly. Her voice was efficient, like a travel agent's laying out the itinerary of a difficult route for a demanding customer. She had planned to go west with my father. She thought she might use her skills by opening a small bakery. But his death took the wind out of her sails. She was moving to St. John's, to an apartment. She would take up a few interests. She had friends there, old school chums who had moved away from St. Patrick's years ago. She was going to sell the house, if anyone wanted it.

"I want it," I heard myself say, "I'll buy it."

She looked at me strangely.

"For the summers," I said. "I need a quiet spot for the summers."

"It's not quiet here, Lily. ATVs on the roads. People speeding all hours of the night. Rowdy youngsters."

I said nothing. Sometimes the best way to clinch a deal is to be absolutely still. I looked at my hands.

"Okay," she said at last, sounding tired, "you can have it."

And I reached out my hand and we shook on it.

Sarah Mellon calls, interrupting my dinner. I have cooked it myself, having made a New Year's resolution to microwave fewer cardboard boxes as a way of sustaining life. I watch my marinara congeal on the counter.

"Lily? I just thought I'd touch bases. You're not coming anymore, are you?"

"No, I don't think so, Sarah."

"I had a feeling about it. I sensed you were uncomfortable. You felt it was all a bit too new-agey for you, didn't you, Lily?"

A fibre optic network carries my fierce colour right to Sarah's house.

"No, Sarah, it's not that—"

"Well, I sensed you were uncomfortable. It's okay. I hope you benefitted in some way from being in the group. Please feel free to come back."

"I will—feel free, I mean."

"Lily, I just wanted to ask you—"

"Sorry, Sarah, I've got to go. My dinner's getting cold."

"Oh, sorry. Bad timing. Well, then, 'bye Lily."

"'Bye." Mercifully. Before I blubber out an apology for not sharing.

I put the cold dinner on the floor. "Here," I say to the cat who has been watching it all along, "*Bon appetit.*"

I wrap myself in layers of fleece and go out into the night. Small city, all clapboard and dead-end streets, with lights not bright enough to dim the stars. There they are, magnificent and sharp and pointy. *New-agey*, I think, *old-agey*, Sarah's world and mine, those differences.

On a November day, clear and shining, a plane passes over a small place in Newfoundland. The pilot sees a snaking line of people, the roads filled with them, some kind of procession. He never forgets this image, or learns its meaning, and he never sees it again, although when he is old it is the prevailing image in his dreams. The processions themselves disappear from this part of the world. How to explain all this to you, Sarah?

I enter the park where I sit on a bench some nights and just look at the stars. Making my mind as clear and sharp as they are. Practising staying awake.

Night Sky Falling

*L*ights. Lights travel around the walls, a circle sweeping my bed. Lights from cars. More cars now all the time, now with the oiled road and the bridge fixed across the river to Cemetery Cove where the pirates' graves are. I watch the lights. In the dark, dark night, in my black room where monsters uncurl among the flowers on the curtains, I hear the pull and swish of tires on oiled, tarred gravel, the spray of rocks let go against the fence. I watch for the lights. The lights are my sworn protectors, for a moment showing the curtains just the way they are, starched cotton covered in dahlias the colour of bruises. The dahlias in real life are the size of bakepots; in the dark they fill my eyes with scaly heads and forked tongues.

In the sudden light, I can see my jammas, beige flannelette with cowboys on horses chasing Indians whose hair is long like mine. Before I can look closely, see all the details of the pink room changed by the dark, before I can make out the lumps like feet in the shadows by the door, before I can find the source of the breathing that comes from behind the toybox, the light is gone. I hold my breath, waiting for the next car to pass, and then before the cowboy on my elbow can shoot the Indian above my left wrist, the darkness covers me in again and I can hear myself—and the other thing—breathe.

I was reading about the sky falling until it got too dark. Chicken Little finds it out and goes and tells everyone. The sky is falling, and what happens next? The whole crowd follows him—Henny Penny, Cocky Locky, the whole lot of them—and none of them asks: how could the sky fall? Stupid book, only for babies, but they're the only kind I have and the Bookmobile won't be here for two weeks.

If I could read myself to sleep, it wouldn't be so bad. But my room's not wired yet. Not finished. Downstairs is, but not up here. There's a thing in the ceiling like a great eye, and from it uncoils the tentacles of a serpent. By Christmas, Mom tells me, the whole house will have electricity. I tell her I want three hundred and sixty-five books for Christmas, one for every day of the year.

Meantime, the dark makes its own game. I wait for the cars, knowing some by their sounds, by what parts are broken or missing. Like this one coming now. No muffler, and he spins his tires, sending tarry rocks into the rhubarb bed. Must be Paul, and soon I will hear the door and fast steps on the stairs and Harrie will go to bed. During the brief swish of circling light, I count all my dolls in the corner. Five dolls. Harriet's getting braver about Dad finding out. She's not allowed to go out with boys who only want one thing.

She'll get a smack if he catches her. She says she don't care. She says she's gone next year. *Bite my dust Dad*, she told him the last time he bawled her out. *Bite my dust, I'll be movin' that fast.*

But Mom always says to Aunt Christa "something's goin' to happen to poor Harrie, and you know what I mean." In their voices full of secrets, the women talk about things by leaving most of the words out. Like Mom's talking about someone over in the Cove. "And her like that. And him. And him with his troubles enough already. And what about the poor youngsters?" And Aunt Christa knows just what she means. "Yeah, yeah, Clara," she says, in her voice that sounds like she's saying the

Sorrowful Mysteries, "but what can anyone do? Sacred Heart of God, the whole lot of them are like it. Her mother, too." Some things you just can't figure out. Some things, Mom says when I ask her too many questions, "you wouldn't want to anyway." Like the sky falling, smack on your head, on an ordinary bright morning.

"You tortured her," I say to him now that she's locked away behind a door she shut herself.

He sets his mouth in a hard line and makes a fist.

"You can't say you didn't. You tortured her."

"It was *in* her," he says. "She tortured herself." The fist, full of withered knots like old rope, smacks into the other hand.

I think I'm going to get to stay up but I'm sent to bed. Peyton Place is coming on. Hildy Ryan says you should go to confession every time you watch Peyton Place. She puts on her sweater with the beaded Shasta daisies on the shoulders, puts her tortoise-shell pins in her bun, in case the crowd on TV can see her, and comes over to watch. Saturday, you can hear her confessing her badness to Father Collins all over the church.

It's not Harrie in the car tonight. It's Dad. I can hear his voice, but it's strange, like he's talking with something thick or sticky in his mouth. He sounds like he's lost in a heavy fog, but from my bed I can just make out the sky—clear, moonless. This is so strange. I get out of bed and creep over to the window, kneel and peep from around the curtain. The smell of meadowsweet, heavy and savory, comes in on the breeze and carries the voices up to me.

His face is pressed against the half-open window of the car, and his mouth is moving, but he is having trouble with the words. I can hear him fiddling with the door handle. Cliff Brake is at the wheel, and he's talking to Mom in his heavy Cemetery Cove accent. "Now, don't go get in a state, Clar'. A man gotta have a bit of a time now an' agin. S'not like a woman. A man gotta have a drop after he's workin' so hard."

"A drop," she says, her voice ice water. "Must be more than a drop in him."

"C'mon," Dad says, "gimme a hand, Clara."

"I knew you were on it. With him. Your buddy. People talk." Each ball of words is like a spit. I can't see her there just inside the gate, but I know she's folding her arms outside her white cardigan. She's got it over her shoulders, buttoned at the neck, and her sleeves are hanging down like a second pair of arms. None of the arms will help him. I hear her footsteps up the gravelly yard. I don't hear him until I am almost sleeping, and I hear a match strike in the dark.

The next day they don't speak. She lets his rashers get cold—deliberately—on the window sill, the window open. When he complains, she says she forgot she put them there she had so much on her mind. Helpless, I watch the big blue flies pitching on his potatoes. If we were like the families on the television, I would fix all this. I'd make them laugh and they'd look at each other. I suppose I should go and hug one of them, but who would I hug?

I'm so down in the dumps I steal ten cents and go buy ice cream and eat it in the curved arm of the gully by Mary Barron's house. I'm not supposed to buy this ice cream, on account of the woman in the shop being in the San one time with TB, but I don't care. Now even if I don't listen to Peyton Place through the heating vent over the stove, I'll have to go to confession anyway.

There are blue dragonflies in the gully, and ferns all up the sides. Nana finds me there and takes my hand, and in silence we walk up to my house. She says to me, "Here, take this dollar now and go get us three bottles of lime crush." And she says to my mother, whose face is all screwed up, "What did you think he'd be like, tell me that. Once they're like it, it always comes back on them. He can't help it. It's *in* him."

Lights. Lights travel around the walls, making patterns like baskets. I count my books. It's late and he hasn't come home. She asks how can he work after being out half the night, but he says there's no fish anyway, so what about work? Three nights now, and him staggering home late. Uncle Fred is home from Churchill Falls, and Dad goes there every night and drinks and Fred talks about all the money he makes. Mom says they're acting like idiots because it's Come Home Year, and all the ones who moved away and got good jobs are home showing off. Sometimes on the roads, you can see the strange women with their Come Home Year 1967 bandannas, words and bridges and roads all over their heads.

Mom walks the floor and watches television with the voice turned down, so it sounds like the crowd on it are in confession. Last night I dreamt I heard her crying.

"You always took her side," he says. We stand facing the greeny glare of the emergency waiting room, its late-night patrons in hasty, unmatched outfits.

"You *never* did," I say.

How could they all have believed it: Goosey Loosey, Drakey Lakey, and Ducky Lucky? Maybe that's what Dad means by *dumb animals*. How could the sky be falling? But in the end, everyone believes. Like around here. You only have to start a story; the rest gets made up along the way, then it's so big a story it must be true. They're saying Harrie's going to have a baby. I heard them. But she's not. I know. What odds about the trip Mom and her took to the doctor. "Time will tell," I say, saucy as you like, to the cluster of women hanging over the counter in Dominic Murray's store.

I'm really not afraid of the dark. But I have a hard time getting to sleep. Once, before the electricity, we'd all be home after dark. Now, Harrie's out all the time and Dad's out and Mom turns all the lights out except for the TV, and the kitchen shimmers blue and you'd think she'd want some company, but she drives me to bed. The other night she smacked me with a wet dishrag when I wouldn't go. I laughed because she can't smack hard. Through the vent, the kitchen is blue like it must be deep under the sea. "She's fully submerged, Captain!" Mom is submerged in the blue kitchen. And she never wears lipstick anymore.

He and I are forced together these days, spending more time with each other than either of us wants to. It makes our nerves jangle like torn wire; sparks fly off us. My hair crackles with static.

"Well, what do you think?" he asks. "Is she any better?"

"No."

"At least she's no worse."

"I suppose that's what you'd call the bright side of it."

"Last night she knew who I was."

"Did she? That must be nice for you."

"I never thought you'd turn out to be the hard one."

"What do you expect? Expect me to be nice to you? Don't forget: you're the one—ones—you and her—who made me the way I am."

"She told me to eff off," he says. "She never said that before. She was a lady when I met her."

The nights are hotter now. Summer's here, and school's over next week. And I wonder what marks I'll get. Or if I'll get a prize. The Grade Threes are getting holy pictures, but the Grade Twos are getting little pins for their jackets; their teacher told them. I want a little pin. The house is full of pictures of Jesus with his heart out in his hand and Jesus as the little lamb (Mary had a little lamb) and Jesus robed as the Infant of Prague. And I'll be promoted to Grade Two. And next Monday we'll go down to the beach. And then it'll be warm enough to swim. And then I'll be seven.

Dad said yesterday that for all anybody cared about him, he might as well go to Churchill Falls with Uncle Fred. He said he might get a good cooked meal in Churchill Falls, and someone to talk to him. He says no one talks to him *in this house.* How come when she's mad, we're all mad? he asks. What has she been telling the youngsters?

"I'm not a youngster," says Harrie. "But Vonnie is. You shouldn't be fighting around her. She has bad dreams."

"I do not. And I'm not a youngster."

"Put some clothes on, Harriet," Dad says, "if you don't mind."

"This *is* clothes!"

"A skirt up to your arse."

"It's the style."

"You're not going out like that."

"Just try and stop me."

"Don't say arse in front of Vonnie," Mom cuts in.

"I'm going over to Fred's."

"Take *her* with you. Take her for a little walk," Mom says, pointing at me.

When we get to Fred's house, Dad asks me to sit on the steps because there are men in there with beer, and some of them are loaded. I sit and watch the red sun drown in the ocean. It takes a long time. When the sun sets, I'll have to go home and go to bed. Uncle Fred is saying, "Aw, Robbie boy, don't go worryin' about it. I pays them no mind. Women's all alike in the end. All right as long as they knows when to keep their mouths shut. But in the end—in the end tis all nag, nag, nag. All of them. From the la-ti-dah lady to the biggest slut in the world. It's all nag, nag, nag some poor man in the end. Even that little girl you got there now, Robbie. Sweet little thing. You'd never say to look at her now, but in the end she'll be givin' some poor fellow grief."

I get my marks: first place in class. For a prize, a picture of Mary with the moon at her feet, and sparkly stuff around her head. It's got a little stand on it, and I put it on the dresser. The sparkly stuff shines in the moonlight, twinkly like real stars. The house has been dead quiet. Mom went to bed at nine o'clock; said she had a sick headache. I heard her throwing up before she went to lie down. I'm wondering what they'll get me for my birthday, when I hear him come home. He's different tonight; he's like a man with a crutch, stumbling and groping for the stairs. He's saying things to himself, his voice rising and falling just like he's talking to another person. I count seconds, then minutes, and he's stuck somewhere on the stairs. I can hear his breath, like someone running. Like Nana's bronchitis. Like a frightened horse. Something tells me tonight's different. No matter how bad he's been lately, he's always been able to walk. After I wait forever, he rasps his way to their room. The springs scringe. "Wake up," he's saying, "Wake up, Clara, wake up."

"For Christ's sake, Rob, what's the matter?"

"Where's my supper?"

"Your supper? Supper's over long ago. I put yours in the oven."

"It's all dried up. Would you expect a man to eat that after a hard day's work? Fry up a bit of fresh meat for me. That's a good girl. Like we used to—"

"We're not like we used to be. Or can't you see at all? You're loaded. Oh . . . the smell of you. Jesus, fish and gurry and beer. Get off my clean bed!"

"Your bed!" he growls and that's when I hear it. I hear a rustle of sheets, the sound of quick movements, then Mom screaming. "No, no!" And then something else again, a sound like a ball being caught by a wet mitten. Then "Oof!"—Mom crying out, not like any sound I've ever heard before, just "Oof!"—then silence. And then he's out of the room, stumbling, his fists pounding the walls, him yelling, "My house! My house! The walls I put up with my own two hands. The roof I nailed on! My house!" His hands pound my door. "I made this door!" and I cringe, hiding, he will kill me for being here—in *his* house, *his* bed, *his* girl who will become a nag. "Jesus! Jesus! Jesus! My house! Built with my own hands! I could tear it down with my own hands. I could burn it to the ground with you all in it if I wanted!"

Sometime during the night the house falls silent. Hiding under the blankets, I listen for every sound. Rain is falling softly, then wild like stormy tears, and a gale that means no fishing blows in somewhere near morning.

The next day, everything has changed. I can't put my finger

on it, but something's different. Mom sits by the window in her best robe, the pale blue chenille one she saves in case she has to go to the hospital. She boils me an egg, and then does no more housework. She only stares out the window, across the road, past the hedge of wild roses where men with brown paper bags full of rattling bottles come and go at Uncle Fred's. I know Dad's not over there because I half-woke early and heard the shed hinges and the scrape of spade on sprong that meant he was going up to weed the potatoes.

"Come here, Vonnie," she says finally, and I think she will explain to me, tell me what happened last night. I go and make myself small and limp in the crook of her arm. But she only says, "Vonnie, you're going to have a new baby brother or sister. Would you like that? You'll have to be a big girl now and help me out."

I'm staring out the window sideways like my head is stuck.

"Yvonne, my love, you'll be happy about it, won't you?"

"Yes," I say. "I'll be happy about it."

Talk all around the stores is that Dad's going to go away with Uncle Fred. I want him to go, want him to go to Churchill Falls where everything is perfect and there are no nags, but he doesn't. Uncle Fred packs his guitar and closes up the house. Harrie goes to St. John's. She says she's just got to get a summer job, or she'll die.

Lights. Lights travel around my room, magic-lantern lights from the cars. Sometimes a car slows right down and a fellow makes kissy-kissy noises at a girl walking the road. I count the shadows and all the clothes in my closet. I'm not afraid of the dark anymore, but I can't sleep. The wind whistles through the curtains with the stupid dahlias, and the rain comes in, taps on the floor. I wonder which car will bring him home, and I wonder will he fight tonight or will he go to sleep? Most nights now he's kind of quiet. It's the garden party dance tonight, and it's the first year she hasn't gone. "My dancing days are over," she said to me this afternoon. She stroked the new navy dress she'd ordered, packed it in brown paper to send it back to the catalogue. He stood there with his lips all white, but she never said a word to him. They only speak now when they're having a racket.

"These trips," he says, "got me wore out."

"Well," I say, "You don't have to come so often. She doesn't mind. She doesn't really know, sometimes."

"She sings, they told me. Sings to herself. Imagine—Clara singing. Perhaps she's happy after all."

"Anyway, that's what we want to believe, isn't it?"

"What?"

"Why don't you say it? Why don't you say you'll be glad when it's over?

"No, I won't. I won't be glad. You don't know."

"Anyway, I'm worn out, too. Let's go to the house and get something to eat. The children'll be up yet."

There are clouds in the sky of his eyes these days. It's hard to hate someone who's just so damn weak.

Once there were Mom and Dad and Harrie and Vonnie. They went on picnics and to the beach. Sometimes, Vonnie's dad would hug Vonnie's mom, and everyone would giggle. Vonnie's mom would blush. Vonnie's mom always wore lipstick because marriage is no excuse for letting yourself go. Remember, girls! Vonnie and Harrie did perfect in school and won prizes. Dad fished, and the family ate some of the fish and sold the rest.

I can't get that story of the dumb animals out of my head,

even though I'm reading long books now. How stupid to believe that the sky was falling! I kept waiting for the end, waiting for them to discover that the sky is only air and water; it can't fall, because it's really nothing at all. Or I'd think: the king can't be an idiot, he's a king. But instead they walked right into the fox's trap, right into his jaws and that was the end of them! I hate stupid stories where you can't change the ending to something sensible.

Besides, if the sky was going to fall, it would fall at night, smother us in our beds. Sometimes at night you can feel the sky coming closer and closer to you. You can't trust the night at all. It makes people different. And then in the day people straighten out their faces, and you'd never say anything ever happened. You can't say anything; you might as well think you had a bad dream.

Mom's knitting, she's hard at it. She's knitting tiny blue and yellow sweaters; I can hear the click-clack of her fast needles half the night. Last week I heard her tell Nana that, maybe if she had a boy this time, everything would turn out all right.

A Notice of Passage

*D*arry Doyle passed away last week. You may have seen the obituaries. They were printed in newspapers in St. John's, Vancouver and New York and, I have heard, in the bulletin of our Lady of the Sorrows Parish which contains that small parcel of cove and cliff and river valley where Darry and I grew up.

"Streeled up," a certain neighbour might have said about us. She didn't approve of children who streamed from house to house, collecting bread and jam and rashers, walking down in the cool dusk from somewhere upriver as if just hearing their mothers' voices, voices that called from front or back steps, that darted through the twilight like raucous birds, growing louder as the dark fell, bothering everyone.

On a three-year-old copy of the *World Almanac*, I draw a diagram, connecting Vancouver, New York, St. John's and our little town, places where Darry burned brightly until he burned out. And I think of Darry "passing away peacefully," as it said in the obituaries, although I dislike euphemisms. But Darry may indeed have passed away, become somehow different, smaller and diaphanous, able to shift shape and disperse slowly through a kind of curtain between this world and the next. How few people know that Darry Doyle had shifted shape before! Had become a saint, or at least something otherworldly. I know because I was there.

Darry grew up next door to me and was my best friend. He spent as much time as he could at our place, especially when the

25

war at his house flared in sudden resurgences of old animosities. Darry was pale and small and had translucent skin, and he could run very fast. My mother was always trying to slow him down and feed him. When he'd skedaddle into our house sideways, he'd rush in as if the wind had blown him and plop down in front of the television as if the gust had just dropped him there. "Me dad's at it again," he'd say. "The Germans are over at the house again. What have you got for supper?"

We'd sit in front of the television, shoulders together, pretending not to listen to the sounds coming from next door. But we would close our eyes and picture what was going on. A bang, the hassock skidding across the room. Darry's father would be behind the chesterfield, his hands shielding his head while shells from twenty years before rained down around him. Darry and his six brothers and sisters would all have run to other houses by then. Darry's mother would be behind the chesterfield too, talking softly to Mr. Doyle until the war subsided, leading him to armistice by describing the details of the room, telling him that the year was 1964, grounding the year in events and details—politicians in office, songs on the top ten, the price of tea. She'd say, "Mary, Angela, Tommy, Cathy, Rodney, Peter, Darry—think of them, will you, Henry," the names of his seven children repeated like a prayer. Darry and I had witnessed all this once. I'd been transfixed, couldn't move a limb, and Darry had had to pull me out of the room. He couldn't stand it. It scared Darry the way time broke down, the way it pulled his father across its borders.

"Shell-shocked." That's how older people described Mr. Doyle. We weren't to make fun of him the way we sometimes did when a person showed himself to be a bit odd. Mr. Doyle was the way he was because he had fought for democracy; fought, our parents reminded us, so that children like us could live without fear.

It was because of men like Mr. Doyle that Darry and I could wander anywhere and all day, safe from the evil Nazis. On the river bank in the slow summer afternoons, we would lie on our stomachs and dump out the contents of our rucksacks. From mine would emerge the heel of a loaf of bread, a piece of rattrap, apples, a small doll I carried everywhere, two tin soldiers, and a small candy box for putting treasures in. Then Darry would dump his loot, and out of his bag would come a cowboy on horseback, an Indian in full headdress riding a palomino, raisins and boiled eggs, a string with a hook for catching fish, never-used, and a book called *Saints for Young Children* which Darry carried everywhere.

We'd assemble our cast of characters on the grass, the Indian, the cowboy, the soldiers and the doll. Sometimes they would all be on an expedition to a new part of the world where no one had ever lived before. Darry would squint and look upriver and say:

"Through the mists over the river, they ride, taking turns on the horses, to the new place."

And I'd say, "Day after day, night after night."

"Until . . . until . . . they have almost no food left."

"Then they arrive in the valley. It is the most beautiful place they have ever seen."

"It is full of—vegetation. It is very green. They got a book with them that tells them what plants are good to eat and what ones are poison. There's tons of berries."

"They won't have to kill any animals for food. No rabbits."

"They won't kill anything."

"Maybe fish, though?" I say hopefully, thinking of the sweet pink flesh of trout.

"No, Marie," Darry says very seriously, "they won't kill anything. Remember: they fought in the war for democracy."

"And they won?"

"Yep, they won. But everything got all torn up. The land and everything."

"So they won't fight no more."

"No. They won't kill anything."

And then, when the valley had grown populous with the children of the new settlers, and the temporary shelters were replaced with houses of river stone that would never burn down, and as the happy citizens dined on wild cress and mint and chanterelles and blueberries, Darry and I would eat our lunches and pore over the pages of *Saints for Young Children*. We would look deep into those unearthly eyes, always turned to a vision of heaven. We would look at the hands, hands so tame birds landed on them and fed, hands marked by holy stigmata, hands that lifted the diseased and the dying from the fetid streets of old Europe, hands that dared raise spears against dragons, and did so without fear.

"I wonder if anyone becomes a saint now," Darry would say.

"Mom's Aunt Ann. She became a saint."

"What did she do?"

"I don't know if she did anything special. But Mom told me about it. Mom saw it. When Aunt Ann died—she was about ninety—her bedroom filled up with the smell of flowers, and there was a lovely smile on her face. And a white rose blossomed in the garden, in December. In the snow. They cut off bits of her hair for relics."

"That's probably just an old story. You have to do something special to become a saint."

"If you could be a saint, Darry, which one would you be?"

He looked at the pictures, studied the beatific faces. "I don't know. I wouldn't want to fight dragons. Or the devil."

"Sshhh, don't even say his name. It's getting dark. I'll be scared to death."

But Darry did become a saint. It happened in the summer of 1965, when Darry and I were nine.

That summer, a year older, taller, braver, we pushed the limits of the expedition farther upriver. Out of sight of the houses now, where not even a wisp of wood smoke showed to suggest homes and families, the great trees rose on both sides of the river. And the river itself widened, grew tributaries pushing long, blue fingers into the country. Up there, in the deep silence, there was a swimming hole called the Bottomless Pool, and beyond it, not far from the river's edge, a family of robins had made their nest.

Darry and I swam in the Bottomless Pool in the mornings and in the late afternoons. In the middle of the day, when the air and the water were warmest, Darry and I wouldn't go near the pool because it would be full of big boys, splashing and shoving and swinging out over the water on ropes tied to trees, yelling like Tarzan as they fell. There was Scar-Thomas, named for the big scar on his forehead where his head caught on a plank when he fell through the wharf. There was Big Henry, almost six feet tall even though he was only eleven. There were Rocky and Bull and Sam the Man. There were Rickster the Trickster and Bang, You're Dead. In the schoolyard they were dangerous enough; near water, they could be deadly. They would haul down your pants and laugh at your skinny butt. They would snap back your wet swimsuit, then let it go so that your eyes watered from the sting. In the pool, they'd call you, "Come 'ere and I'll drown you, you little fart." They would hold you underwater with their knees clasped tight around your ears.

While the big boys swam, Darry and I hid in the woods and watched the robins. We'd watched the building of the nest, seen the unbelievable pale blue of the eggs, heard the first calls of the new birds. Now the nestlings were bigger and stronger and were making their first attempts at flight. When Darry and I watched them, time disappeared. Five minutes or an afternoon might pass. We were under a kind of spell.

"Ah, look at this, Sammy, the babes in the woods." It was Scar-Thomas. "What are ya at?"

"Givin each other a poke, I daresay," said Sam the Man, "checkin out their parts."

The boys laughed.

"Watchin the baby birdies," said Thomas.

"I wonder what they taste like?"

"What?"

"The birdies. Can you eat them? Wouldn't be much of a feed, though." It was Bang, You're Dead, shinning up the tree, hauling on the branches around the nest.

"Leave em alone." Darry's voice was small and high and cold.

"What did you say, you little sissy?"

"I said, leave em alone."

And Darry jumped and landed against Bang You're Dead's legs, and he pulled, and the others moved in like a wave breaking, and everything happened the way it does in a dream, oddly, in slow motion.

What I could see was a mass of bodies, limbs flailing. The sound of punches. Blood sprayed out into the air; I saw its mist pattern my hand. There was yelling and cursing, and Darry was in the middle of it all, and nobody could hold him. He fought with his arms and his legs and butted with his head. All the parts of his body had become sudden weapons. And he was making a strange sound, a kind of growling. Then the big boys were running, crashing through the trees. Someone screamed, "Jesus, he almost tore me arm off!"

And then there was only Darry and me, him crumpled on the ground, soundless, still. Dead, I thought. I was afraid to go near him, and I waited for a long time, during which I heard the ticking of my watch and a trout leap out of the pool. Then I knelt down by Darry. I thought about how to get his body back home, of what I'd say to his parents. I thought about wild animals waiting to feed on his body, of the boys waiting in the woods to finish me off. I wondered if they'd beat me the way they beat Darry, or if they'd carry me back to the pool and drown me there.

Then Darry said, "What happened? What time is it?"

And when I looked, he was sitting up. His face was pale and unmarked, and a kind of light seemed to glow around him. "I'm a bit sore," he said. "What happened?"

I couldn't speak.

"I got in a fight, I think. Mom'll kill me."

But I couldn't speak. I couldn't speak because he was standing up, brushing leaves off himself, when his legs should be broken, and his rib cage smashed, when blood should have run from his ears and mouth and nose, when his eyes should have been swollen shut and dead inside. Now that he was, instead, standing, unhurt except for a small cut on his right forearm, what could I say?

You were made into something different, Darry, you scared me, a voice said inside my mind. But my mouth said, "You gave a lot worse than you got."

Darry sat down again and looked at the tree with the nest in it. I opened my nose for the smell of suddenly blooming flowers, watched for the smile of beatification I'd seen in Darry's book. There was nothing like that but I knew that I had seen a transformation, and it made me go all quiet inside. I would have liked to ask Darry about it, to ask if he'd felt something happen, a great heat or cold or a strange feeling deep in his cells, something that told him that the very make-up of his body was changing.

I didn't ask, though. We picked up the spilled contents of

our rucksacks and went home. There was no need for Darry to ask me not to breathe a word of what had happened to his parents. But I couldn't keep my eyes off the one small cut he'd received.

Later, when the cut healed, it left a scar in the shape of a bird.

I never told anyone about the fight in the woods. The big boys told no stories either; they had no words, no past experiences, around which to build such a story. It would always remain one of those moments when time stops, and the world becomes unknowable, indescribable. *Something weird went on*, they'd say, we'd say later if we said anything at all.

Many people in the art world have tried to puzzle out the origins of Darry Doyle's unusual clocks. I have said nothing, but I always knew. If it was Darry's fate to grow up in near-silence, to hold something within him that would cause him to become a maker of beautiful, unusual objects, then the fight by the river was the moment out of time when the clocks began. You have probably seen them, been struck by their unusual grace in a gallery or in the home of someone who could afford one.

I have one here in this room. It was a gift or, rather, a trade for services in the design of a garden. My clock gives me the sense of time melting, the face tilted, just slightly off a perfect oval, a warped egg, close enough to a perfect shape to draw attention to the deliberate act of distortion. The legs are thin, appear to be giving up under time's weight, slender zig-zagged legs of wrought iron. Such clocks keep the time we have forgotten or deeply secreted.

You have perhaps also seen the bowls. You may be fortunate enough to own one. Valleys hammered out of the many metals Darry experimented with. Fine etchings along the valley floor, and up the sides. Rivers, trees, reeds. Sometimes, shapes vaguely human breaking through the great inland woods to the river valley, the place of new settlement, the place beyond war.

The last time I saw Darry I said I wanted to buy a bowl, and Darry insisted that he choose one for me. "I'll send it to you." he said. He'd been home for a visit, seeing his mother. He didn't look well, but he was full of a strange, unpredictable energy that surged and ebbed. He had been HIV positive for so many years that the first symptoms of AIDS had managed to catch him by surprise. On one warm day after he returned from seeing his mother, he accompanied me on a drive outside the city to the country house of Mrs. John Q. Beech, as she refers to herself. Mrs. Beech is my most difficult client.

I design, or I should say, re-design gardens. Usually, it's the latter. People will begin with their own ideas, with truckloads of earth, flats full of transplants and dreamy gardening books originating in the kinder climate of the south of England. And things will turn out wrong. Then they'll call me to fix the problem. They expect miracles.

I have taken Darry along because of the sunshine, the breeze, the car's open windows, and because the drive to Mrs. Beech's house winds around a large pond where terns are nesting. And because the visit to his mother had plunged him into silence.

"What does the Q stand for?" Darry asks.

"I don't know. Quibbling? Querulous? Not quotidian, for sure."

Darry laughs. "I picture a Dowager Empress of Topsail," he says. "What's our great gardening challenge today?"

"Edges," I say. "No, don't ask. You'll see."

Mrs. Beech is waiting by a rose bush that has a tendency to be expansive. It is Mrs. Beech's notion that my job is to make plants conform to some very precise ideas she has about space. I can do this if I have to; one only has to be ruthless. But it is hard for me to be this way, because it is not what I believe about gardens. I believe that growth fills in the open-ended questions in a living design, and that boundaries are made to be crossed, perhaps obliterated.

I introduce Darry, and she immediately defers to him, as if, being a man and tall, he is some expert I have brought in to solve finally the problems of edges and borders.

"Look," she says, "come here," grabbing his elbow and moving him along to a curved stone pathway. She points to the edges. "You see," she says. "This is the problem. Marie simply won't see it. Everything is spilling over the edges. Everything is going wild. It will just be a tangle if we don't take decisive action. You can't make out the edges of things."

"How fortunate you are to have such good soil," Darry says.

"What?" Mrs. Beech asks, offended but intrigued. Across the path, I'm checking the drip-irrigation system and straining to listen. I expect Mrs. Beech to do something rough and antiquated, box Darry's ears perhaps.

"Well," says Darry, "You're very lucky to have such good soil. After all, it's often pretty thin around here."

"Well, I had it put it in myself, didn't I. It cost me a fortune." Her arms flutter up, describing in the air a huge moneybag.

"And now, you have made such rich soil your plants can't contain themselves. Such exuberance! It's beautiful."

"But the edges. We worked so much on the shape . . ."

Darry appears to be talking to himself. "I wonder what edges are for, if they are not to be crossed. Hidden. Overcome."

Mrs. Beech is silent. You can sense in the still air an intimation that she is holding Darry's idea, turning it around, attracted to it, trying to separate expertise from bullshit. But she recovers, "Well, that's not what I'm paying for, is it, though?—some idea of the infinite."

Still, before we leave, she gives him an armload of the renegade roses.

"People love to have you try to fool them, Darry," I tease as we drive back to St. John's.

I sense the way the other side of the car plunges into darkness. I know I have said something so absolutely wrong that I must not prolong the misery by trying to take it back.

Darry's obituary has appeared in newspapers in St. John's, New York and Vancouver, a kind of odd, pulled kite shape superimposed over the map of North America. Before this notice of passage reached the parish bulletin circulated in that small place where Darry and I began, one line was excised. I heard Mrs. Doyle cut it out herself. The line read, "In lieu of flowers, donations may be made to the Valley of Peace Hospice." Darry's house, which he opened to everyone. But the line travelled anyway, tucked under the arm of a candy salesman who left the newspaper on a convenience store counter. Such news always travels.

And Mrs. Doyle had to face it, that her son's beautiful house had become a space for the dying, that the wife she'd invented for him, who never visited because of her complete terror of air travel, had not existed. There was, after all, no mention of her in any obituary. And Mrs. Doyle, who had had to repeatedly put an end to the Second World War in her living room, had to forge yet another kind of armistice. Another treaty between sorrow and shame.

Since Darry passed away, I have begun to feel older although I am not yet forty, and he will never be. Over and over, I think of those days when we were small and warmed by the sun together on the river bank. And I think with regret of those years of late adolescence and early adulthood when I wouldn't speak to Darry at all because of an abject humilation I'd brought on myself.

The year we were fourteen, I thought now was the time for Darry and me to be boyfriend and girlfriend. It was the most natural thing in the world; how could I ever be so close to anyone else? So I dressed for him, and thought of him as I ringed my eyes with navy-blue eyeliner, and practised sending him messages he didn't want to receive out of what I imagined to be their sultry depths. I asked him for the last dance, and he always danced it.

One night after one of those high-school dances, we stood on one of the small bridges over the river where we used to play. The moon hung like a scimitar over us. I groped the railing to hold his hand, then felt it stiffen.

"Darry?" I willed him to turn to face me.

I cradled his face in my hands and leaned closer.

"Ah, don't Marie," he said, turning so abruptly my mouth hit his jawbone hard. "Ah, don't."

It was years before we could laugh about this, Darry learning to make a joke of it long before I could. "I was so mixed up, Marie," he said. "My mother was always saying her curtains were gay; I didn't want to be curtains."

I also cannot help thinking about how Darry died. Who was with him? What happened in those last moments? Did the bird in the scar rise from his arm and fly off to nest in the old-growth rainforests of British Columbia? Did he become still and tranquil, undergoing a transformation into saint again? Did he lie waxen and glowing, the way he did on the forest floor the day I wondered how to get his body home, only to hear him rise and speak, back from the dead. There are things I wish to know—what flew out of a certain room, whether a flower suddenly bloomed out of season, whether there is a witness who carries a story for which he or she can find no words.

I take down the bowl Darry chose for me, and trace the bronze figures inside it. In the burnished late evening, sunlight is absorbed in the bowl, a valley at sundown. It is a detailed valley, holding a river with its tributaries, small flats of rich land rising out of it. Through it march two tin soldiers, tired, bent under their packs, and a cowboy with a six-shooter and a coffeepot. On horseback are an Indian in full headdress and a small girl with a doll-like face. If I squint, I can enlarge the valley and give the small figures flesh and breath.

Through the mists over the river, they ride, taking turns on the horses, to the new place. Day after day, night after night. Until they have almost no food left. Then they arrive in the valley. It is the most beautiful place they have ever seen. It is full of vegetation. It is very green. They can tell from a book they have which plants are good to eat, and which are poison. And there are tons of berries, too. They won't even have to kill any animals for food. No rabbits. They won't kill anything, except possibly fish. No, not even that; they won't kill anything.

Before they got to the valley, they fought in the war for democracy. And they won. They won, but everything got all torn up in the war. The land and everything. So they won't fight anymore. They won't kill anything.

And then the valley grows populous with the children of the new settlers, and they build houses out of river stone so that they will never burn down. And they are happy. The valley gives them everything. In the evening, they light small fires and gather to tell stories, to dine on wild cress and mint, chanterelles and blueberries.

Pioneers

*S*torms excite me; I cannot sleep. On this wild night, around midnight, I walk around the house and look out from each of its windows. Through the small pane set in the door to the garden, the forsythia is sculpted like a frozen waterfall. Tufts of dead plants stand in formal sprays, their seedpods glazed. The snow is whispering over the tracks of a stray cat, covering them. In the kitchen, where the moon usually enters via objects of coloured glass—chimes, vases—the window is white with wind-pressed snow, and the light that comes in is almost the same as the moon's light, turning everything blue. I note this, walking through the still living room, how the snow's intensity in this storm has mimicked the full moon, blueing and whitening objects. I think of old washers and rinse cycles. For a moment, I feel that I am in a snow fort, deep in the old garden, a blue-white space, with the world far away from it and supper a sure thing in just a little while more, toutons and molasses or duck soup or fish cakes so full of onions they burn your eyes when you open the porch door.

The living room window is the largest, and I save it for last. But before I reach it, I hear voices. Children's voices. Now what can they be doing out there? I cannot make out the words. From old habits of careful non-involvement, I lift the curtain only a little and slowly, peering out. Two children, swaddled and bent, walking, on each side of a woman, presumably their mother. A scrap of wind throws her voice against the window, against my face, "Sshhh, we'll be there in a second. Don't go bawling." Up the street they go, carried by a wind rushing to erase their footsteps, to some place, I can tell from their sure steps, they have already chosen. And I wonder what the refuge is from. A cold house, the furnace out of oil? An angry man with the storm inside him? And I think of my mother's face in the light of the Aladdin lamp, *Oft I had heard of Lucy Grey . . . She dwelt on a wide moor.* Knowing that moors are like bogs, places of swallowing up and loss and miraculous rescues, we'd sit and imagine the greater terror of storms in open, lonely places, and as sudden as wind can drop, we would feel safe.

My father was working at construction in St. John's the winter that the storm cut us off from the rest of the world. He went in November, right after the fish plant closed, before his first UI cheque even came through. It was strange for us; we were used to him being there all winter, supported by two kinds of cards. One kind of cards he'd fill out and send in the mail, and a while later a cheque would arrive. The other kind of cards he slapped down vigorously in the house next door, long nights over bottles of Dominion, when the out-of-work hands would bang the table so hard bottles would fly straight up and land exactly in the small pools of rime where they'd sat before. A substitute for hammering nails, or weighing fish, this fist on the table. Often he won at cards. He said you couldn't fool him at cards, but I wondered could you be good at forty-fives? What was the skill?

Whatever. Some nights he came home with things—a brace of dead rabbits, a decanter set decorated with the four card suits, a pair of mittens knitted by someone's wife. Once he came home with a dead lamb cradled in his arms. He carried it tenderly, it's head in the crook of his arm, as if it was someone's lost and frozen child he had found in the storm, his face crumpled and sorrowful as if he would have to tell someone very bad news.

Sometimes the cards, the winnings of objects or animals, would not be enough for him. His idle hands would curl and palpate. He would make fists in his pockets. His body would jump as if someone only he could hear had called him. He would tell everyone to go to bed. It was like a weather system inside the house, unstable, always threatening a good blow.

But the winter I was fifteen he was gone. My uncles were busy that year doing the inside finish work on houses they had built in the fall, and my father was a good carpenter. The first weeks he'd come home on Friday, happy and with a paycheque, something changed about him, as if he had grown taller. He'd give us spending money, and go take a long bath because he didn't like to do such a private thing in someone else's house. Then, his hair slicked and combed, in an ironed shirt, trailing Brut someone had given him for Christmas, he'd go out looking for cards or dances, like a young man home from university for the weekend, eager to catch up with his old friends.

Most nights he would come home happy, but sometimes you could just see the world had failed to provide him with a good fight, and there just might be one waiting home in the kitchen.

Like one night he came in, and looked at us in a dark way, my mother asleep on the daybed, her face wrecked by dreams, myself by the stove, my feet in the oven, reading *Great Expectations* for school. He looked at me.

"Whas wrong with you? Not warm enough is it?"

"Oh, it's fine. Finest kind. I just like to sit like this."

He looked at me like I was lying or had used big words on him or said something in a grand accent just to torment him.

"What, not hot enough for ye?" He looked at my mother.

"Couldn't any of ye get up long enough to put a junk in the stove? Well, I'll make it hot enough for ye."

He went to the woodbox, sidling a little. Junk after junk he brought, jamming them in, filling the stove to the bed. Then he forced down the lid, wiggling it with the lifter to close it. "Now, you'll be hot enough," he said. He boiled the kettle. It didn't take long. But his face was full of disappointment as he cut his own bread, spread the blueberry jam on it because there was not a decent woman in the house to make a lunch for him.

The room got hotter. The top of the stove reddened. I had to move my feet out to the edge of the oven door, but still my socks gave off the smell of burning wool. My hands glowed. *Great Expectations* itself was heating up in my hands, the paper dry and giving up the acrid smells of old fibres and ink. I felt that it might catch fire in my hands, Pip's cold, misty world burning. The blood in my body felt superheated, but I wasn't moving until he went to bed. I'd cook first. Finally he went for the stairs. He looked at my mother. His face was strangely twisted, like my grandfather's after his stroke, a smile stuck on one side, and a scowl floating on the other. "Tell her," he said "if she wants to sleep, why don't she go to bed out of it."

We smiled when he came home on Fridays, and sighed with relief when he left on Sunday afternoons, his head swivelling from one side of the van to the other as it went down the road, a last, longing look at the house and the stable as if they might disappear in his absence.

Then the storm hit the week after New Year's, and the stable did disappear for days at a time. It was how we judged how fierce storms were, looking out and saying, "The stable's gone, you can't see across the road." The clothesline went too, snapped and went down on the ground, the load of clothes disappearing under banks of snow. During a lull, I dug out the clothes, frozen bodies with arms and legs extended in odd, appealing gestures, like avalanche victims. We warmed them on a line above the stove, the melting snow hissing on the hot surface below. I was free to do as I pleased now. The bus driver had stopped his futile attempts to get us to the high school in St. Patrick's, a dozen miles of impassable road away.

It was a world full of sound. The hot hiss from drying clothes. The steady singing of tap water in the steel sink, as water had to be kept running so the pipes wouldn't freeze. The crackle and sputter of burning wood, boiling kettles. And except when it stopped for breath, the wind, a howling, bawling wind that seemed to come from every direction at once, wrapping the house in a terrible ballad or ghost story that went on night after night. My mother said the racket would drive her off her head if it didn't stop soon, and I told her about the mistral which I had read about in a book about the climates of the world.

Sometimes the wind would die down around sunset. Then I'd walk out, out of the hot smells of stew and baking bread, digging a path through the yard, the crunch of snow shovels echoing through the first indigo dark, the faint blue light of stars coming out through wind-ripped clouds, the snow responding by giving off a billion blue and golden sparks of its own. In this strangely blessed world of beauty and near silence, I'd go the store and stock up on food and other necessities, and quite a bit of junk food, and charge it all on credit. We had no money. I'd come home and fill the fridge and the cupboards, hand out bars and chips to my younger sisters, a cherry cake for my mother. This last was a peace offering, because my mother would get upset when I didn't ask her what to get. But if I did ask her, she'd say, "I don't care. Get what you like." By the time we'd had our tea and cake, the wind and the drift would have started again.

States of siege feed a great appetite for news. My father's voice crackled over ice-laden phone lines, a little slurred. We wondered if this was a bad connection, or if he was off drinking his earnings at the Old Dory Tavern with the uncles and their buddies. Reassuring him that we were all right, the road would be open soon, we listened for a juke box in the background.

Out of the radio came exceptional announcements. Mrs. Mary Finn had been calling our Member every day, asking him what he was going to do, or was he going to wait until someone died? And there was the Member himself. He knew the situation, he said. He had flown over the area in a helicopter. The road could not be opened until the weather changed. He had seen where a plow had overturned, and the driver had to be rescued. He had seen for himself the cuts made by plows, and a tunnel was how he described it, the walls meeting at the top. Banks fifteen feet high. In other places, you couldn't tell what was road, what was barrens. He spoke as if just seeing all this had been at great personal risk to himself.

He was sending a helicopter to bring out the sick and anyone else who might be in danger. The helicopter would also carry out the Grade Elevens because they had public exams to write in the spring and they couldn't afford to miss school. They would be boarded in St. Patrick's at the government's expense.

On the next fine day, the promised helicopter landed by the gut, and we watched them go, load after load, pregnant women, old people, a small child with pneumonia, his mother carrying him rolled up tight in blankets so that he looked like some monstrous blue grub. Then the Grade Elevens, in three trips, us yelling at them, "Ya poor things!" "Have a good time." and "Do some studying for me, will ya!" Hooting 'cause we were free, although we'd been told to gather in the clinic to study and to do assignments sent over the phone.

"I'm getting pneumonia myself," my mother said from the daybed one evening.

"You're not," I said.

"I am. I can feel it here. Like a wind whistling in my chest."

"You could go out on the helicopter if you're really worried."

"And who'd look after them?" she said, pointing at Jane and Patricia in front of the television, where they were hunched over, trying to see something through the snow on the screen.

"I'd look after them."

"You can't. You're too young."

"I'm not. I do lots of things."

"You think you're old enough, missy. For a lot of things. But you're not. You wait and see."

A gust of wind hit the window behind her head. She ducked as if she expected a fist to come through the glass.

"Your daddy." she said. "Maybe he'll get home soon."

"What do you want him home for? When he's here, you'll want him gone."

"That's not the truth."

"It is. I knows it."

Maybe I was the one who drew out her strength and blew the whistling wind into her chest. As the days went on, my mother got sicker, and I got stronger. The electricity came and went, and in the dark I lit the kerosene lamp and wished we had candles to carry up the dark stairway and into another time. I warmed the old flatiron on the stove and before we went to bed, my sisters and I pulled down the quilts and ironed our sheets before jumping in. My mother slept in the kitchen to watch the stove. Our pipes froze, despite the water-torture drips, and I found out who had water still running and went twice a day to fetch it in scoured galvanized buckets. I boiled eggs and fried slices of ham. And, since our mother had stopped baking, I made sandwiches with soft white baker's bread, sandwich spread and bologna. After digging out the yard, they were the best things I'd ever tasted. There was a tank for warming water on the side of the stove, and I'd fill it with snow, so the next day it would have melted and warmed enough for washing. I did laundry in the sink and hung it over the stove. My mother watched me through half-closed eyes, disapproving. "You," she wheezed, "I don't know what's wrong with you, you're having such a good time when the rest of us are so miserable." The thing in her chest cried out like a tern.

But I was having a good time. I had become a pioneer. One of those girls I read about in novels of the American West, a brave and imaginative provider, a worker and dreamer, one of those strong young women on the covers of novels, their hair windswept, their eyes gazing out in hope and determination over the wild expanses of prairie, the way my eyes gazed out over the frozen dunes of snow. At the end of their work, a kiss waited that would burn in them forever. Or I was one of those brave girls from Newfoundland's past. Like Ann Harvey, who went out in boats with her father when she was only a teenager to rescue the shipwrecked, making a lifeline with her strong, young arms. Or the girl down the shore, a Lucy there was a song about, like Lucy in the poem *on the wild moor*, a girl who walked across the barrens with a lantern to fetch a doctor for her family, all of them but her struck down with diphtheria. There were no more young people like them, my father had said with some bitterness. But I was like them now. I'd cook and clean, carry and fetch, and at night I'd go up to the clinic to study.

The study group was dwindling. Some nights only three or four showed up, mostly girls. Hardly anyone had finished *Great Expectations*. Without boys, the group got duller. And Mickey Morrissey had never showed up at all. He was the one I wanted to be there. With his crow-black hair and matching eyes, and his sauciness about study. We divided up a list of people to call for the next meeting. We decided to tell them to bring snacks and tapes. When? The next night the lights were on. I said I'd call Mickey; no one else wanted to, afraid he'd make fun of them.

Last summer at a party at a place we called Inn Behind the Cliffs, it was so private, Mickey and I had ended up sitting alone on the hill above the beach. Mickey offered to share his beer, but I said, "No, thanks. I don't drink."

"What else don't you do?" he asked.

"I don't know."

"Well, I'll say things and after I say them, you say, *I would* or *I wouldn't.*"

He started. "You'd let me put my arm around you."

"I would."

He did. "You'd let me kiss you."

"I would."

Much later, after my lips had melted and reformed into things of a queer and awkward shape, he said. "You'd stay if I took off my shirt."

"I would." I had to push out the words.

His chest glowed in the moonlight. "You'd let me take off your shirt."

"I would," and shivered.

"You'd let me unhook your bra."

"I wouldn't. I can't."

"Tease. Let me know when you're a woman." And he was off in a spray of rocks that racketed down the cliff face.

"Knock it off, will ya," a voice called up. "Go screw where you won't kill someone."

I lay wrapped in my shirt, red-faced, looking at the sky. It would do no good to tell Mickey that all-seeing Mr. God was in the moon. That in the stars were the eyes of my mother and her celestial counterpart, the BVM. That my father had split himself into a thousand spirit eyes that looked from behind the branches of every spruce tree.

But now when I told him about the study group, the tapes and the snacks, he said. "Sounds like a party."

The night the boys came back to the study group we changed the dialogue in *Great Expectations* to the way things would be said on the shore. We ate chips and drank Coke and danced to the Beach Boys. Mickey extended his hands toward us like some TV performer, and sang, "I wish you all could be California girls." Later, Mickey and I dawdled, hanging about the lane, pretending to be interested in the constellations, until the footfalls died away. On the side of the road there was a depression in the earth which had once been the foundation of a house. We stood in this crater, under a pine tree, and kissed. Then Mickey opened his coat, his shirt. Then mine. Four weeks of storm rushed in. Then we knelt and he unhooked my bra and kissed my nipples. "If it wasn't for the fear of pneumonia . . ." Mickey said as we walked down the lane. I made him stay in the shadows until I got to my gate, alone.

In bed, I lay between the iron-warmed sheets and thought of the winter going on like this, days of all kinds of useful labour, and the nights with Mickey. I pressed my hands in the hot space between my legs and thought of shovelling snow, carrying water and being a woman.

The siege ended the first week of February. One morning when I went out, the sky was a full limpid grey like a gull's wing, and the snow was soft and sticky under my boots. Everywhere there was the soft tap, tap, tap of melt. Diamond drop necklaces hung, swelling on windowframes, then splattered gems. Water dripped onto oil drums, galvanized buckets, sleds. Off eaves onto steps and rails. Off tree branches to the snow, digging for the earth and its dormant shoots and bulbs. A soft sound, yet magnified, a chorus and echo from every house and yard, congregating in the ear.

When the sky let loose, it was a deluge of rain, dense, opaque. It dug out the banks of snow, made curious tracks and paths like those of animals. Rivulets formed, swelled and overflowed, turned into rivers, streaked past the doors of houses on the way to the sea. By the shore, the sea itself was churned, muddy, the earth entering it. Drains and taps whistled and moaned, then let out great gushes of rusty water. "What're ya at?" a man called to his neighbour, who was cutting wood, "Building an ark?" The rain went on for days, unremitting. The air began to clear and with it, my mother's chest. The tern in her lungs cried loudly, and then came the rattling and coughing, the breaking up of flu.

I went out to get away from the awful sound of breaking phlegm, and dug a trench and packed up slush on its sides to give the water a place to run off the main path to the gate. As sure as it was February, it would freeze again soon, and who wanted an ice path to the gate? When I went in, I heard the unmistakable sounds of bread being kneaded and I thought *the times they are a'changin'*.

As the week went on, road crews ploughed through the mess that had once been a road and opened what appeared to be, some people said, a water route to St. Patrick's. The Channel, they called it. The mail came by road for the first time in five weeks. The boarding students came home. And, on Friday evening, the shore taxi pulled up by the gate, and out stepped my father. He blinked and looked around, as if surprised to see the place again, not fallen into ruin or burnt to the ground. He looked around at a shining, ice-sculpture world, where freeze had followed thaw as predictably as it always did. A rose bush glittered at him in the lights from passing cars.

It wasn't long after he got inside that he began to show us the stuff that he was made of. After a lunch, he pulled out his wallet and laid it on the table. "See, here," he said. He laid each bill down as though they were cards in a particularly stunning hand of forty-fives. *One hundred. Two hundred. Three hundred. Four hundred. Five hundred. Six hundred. Seven hundred. Twenty-forty-sixty-*

eighty—eight hundred. And fifty. We didn't say anything, although he kept watching our faces. Anything would have been the wrong thing.

He didn't go look for cards or dancing that night. He went to the store and brought home treats. He watched TV. Jane and Patricia watched too. I sat with my feet on the oven door, reading *Great Expectations* for the third time, having run out of anything else to read, and tired of thumbing the mail-order catalogues with the young ones, imagining ourselves in all the outfits or picturing our bedrooms festooned with lavender priscillas and matching bed canopies.

We had the TV put in a corner of the dining room in such a way that, if you wanted to look straight at it, you had to turn your back to whoever was in the kitchen. So he sat there, with his back turned on my mother, who was on the daybed. Every now and then, she'd ask him a question.

"And how are Richard and Daphne?"

"The finest kind."

"And Jim and Pat?"

"Good."

"And the youngsters—did they get flus?"

"No, tough as anything."

"You're not saying much."

"No."

They were both restless, we all could see that. Jane would catch my eye and smile. My mother kept looking at my father's back, as if in the complicated weave of his sweater there was encrypted some message about why she'd wanted him home and what she'd got. He arsed around on the vinyl seat of the chair, discontented, and while spies chased each other in improbable boats through the glittering canals of Venice, he raised his head and pricked his ears like a horse listening for voices on the road, and craned to see if he could make out who was passing beyond the sheer curtains, their passage announced by the bobbing glow of cigarettes and the low rumble of talk.

By Saturday night he had to go out. Around supper you could see it. The restlessness. Somewhere, cards were doing a gentle shuffle-rustle, soft as a taffeta gown, on a Formica table, and sending him telepathic messages. You would have to tie him to a chair to keep him in the house.

I had to go to school on Monday. I packed the assignments, the books, my hands suddenly devoid of all energy. I looked out at the yard, nearly normal now for February, and wished for work, for a great challenge, for something of use to save. But all I saw on the way to the bus was a frozen cat, a ginger stiffness against the snow. I felt that all the use had gone out of my life and that I'd die before June came and set me free.

Once, in my twenties, I went with my townie lover out around the bay to a summer house that belonged to a friend of mine. But it wasn't summer; it was a Newfoundland April, the sky like a contusion by mid-afternoon, the wind making the small car dance. We missed the turn-off to the community where the house, we were told, sat on a hill at the end of a road where we couldn't possibly miss it. Backtracking, peering at the road map, arguing good-naturedly, we finally arrived there after dark. The wind almost knocked us over as we carried bags and boxes from the car.

The house, "the former residence of a sea captain," had no electricity, no furnace, no flush toilet, no running water. A stream of clear water close by gurgled under a fine skin of fern-patterned ice. An outhouse sat by a shed. Inside, a huge black woodstove half-filled the kitchen, promising warmth, eventually. A kerosene lamp sat filled and waiting on a kitchen shelf. In the downstairs bedroom, a chamber pot wreathed in primroses awaited nocturnal emergencies.

"Everything we need," my lover said. He lit a candle and poured us each a stiff Irish whisky. "No need for ice," he quipped. He held up the kerosene lamp, "Now, how do you get this going?"

I showed him, adjusting the wick, wiping the chimney free of dust, lighting the lamp, watching the room glow in its burnished light.

He was already at the stove, filling and fiddling, a black smoke creeping up in his face.

"You have to adjust the key," I said, "the draught," and went over and did it so that the fire started to draw properly and became more like something that would actually keep a body warm.

"Didn't you have woodstoves in your house?" I asked.

"No, fireplaces." he said.

And I stood there thinking about how we were so different, woodstoves and fireplaces. How he probably grew up in a house where parents, reliably, got up before the children and lit fires and simmered pots of porridge. Where children were not expected to learn the secrets of provision. And I had a vision of myself on a morning in late winter, rising to light the stove, to boil eggs and make toast on a rack held above the lid, warming the house gradually and going off in the sunrise to make the Stations of the Cross before another soul stirred in the house.

"You know how to light fires, though?" I teased.

"I do. I was a Boy Scout."

"A Boy Scout could perish around the bay," I said. "You'll have to rely on me to keep you warm."

We were in that first stage of a relationship where a teasing word, the electricity passed eye to eye, the ghost of a smile would cause us to fall together onto the nearest horizontal surface. And there we were now, laughing, Skipper's old daybed by the stove, too close and too cliched to resist.

All weekend, as we tumbled in and out of bed, as we talked and ate and drank and played cards, and agreed it was too cold to go outdoors for anything but necessity, I stoked fires and tended the lamp. I woke in the middle of the night with the wind rushing by, the sound of an aerial sea, and smelled the warmth rising from his skin and went to check the banked fire to make sure it would keep going all night. Lying there with him, I felt that in this stormy world, this wind-battered place, the lighting of lamps and the banking of fires might turn out to be the greatest acts of love. Although no one had yet mentioned the word *love*; for me, it was only a thing in sonnets.

Tonight, I am so curious about the woman and the children on the street. A veteran of storms, I wonder what brought them out. I think of my mother on the daybed, giving out a few more lines about Lucy: *Her feet disperse the powdery snow / That rises up like smoke.*

I imagine all the possible things that might produce the need to go out into the night. An empty oil tank, that sudden dead cold, by mistake or because there is no money. A sick relative close by, in danger, the sudden phone call. Or something in the house, a domestic incident. And I imagine a house where a man sits now alone at a table playing patience, a man caught between two kinds of cards, with nothing useful to do with his mind or his hands all winter. I see his hands, the way they bend the insubstantial cards with their fickle suits. I see the woman watching his hands and gauging the strengths and resistances of the wind, the walls, her body, the length of the night. I see her invent a need to check on her mother. An emergency that will carry her out into the wind and away from it at the same time.

I put on a coat and step into shoes and go and stand in the

doorway. My eyes track the sets of footsteps, now merely dents in the snow, to the doorway of a house up the street. The house is brightly lit, and I know that the woman and the children are inside. I go in my house, lock my door. Upstairs, the hall light dims and blinks. Upstairs, my townie lover sleeps, still with me after ten years. Our child lies next to him, addicted to her parents' warmth. I consider lighting the woodstove, to bank a small fire in case of power failure. But I abandon the idea. It is too easy to imagine emergencies. I turn out the lights, thinking how these things, warmth and light, though they may still fail, are much more reliable than they were in the past.

Silence

*H*ere is a closed space, closet space. Hidden things, dust and cobwebs, hinted space full of rolled scarves and yellowed forgotten underwear, always too good to wear. Another's house, another's room, another's place, trying to imagine a partner gone and would that be worse than this? Here to clean up, clean out, amongst the boxes, the curtained shelves like confessionals because no one else can stand to be here among her absence and all the things she hoarded. A ghost of dust clinging to the mirror's edge, soft like sponge, liable to float off, a hat hanging cockeyed off the edge where the sponges of dust dip and float, dip and float. Novenas pasted on cards stuck in the mirror frame which should be lined with pictures of the grandchildren her own were too spiteful to give her. How did she pass those sponges of dust, she with her rag permanently attached to her hand—perhaps because they were on the mirror, and she never had the time to look at herself. Floating dust, up, downward—where are the drafts coming from with the house insulated so tight—the mirror corner, the hat of felt.

Felt. What is felt? What in her room, the soft hat or the softer darkness, was felt? Did she rub the hat ever and think of wearing it? Like a caress on her head, a felt kiss. Her friend Marina told her that hats were the cure for depression. On the real dark days, she said, when you can't think what to do, buy a hat for yourself and wear it out to bingo. Darkness covered her like a hat, covers her now.

Once. Then. I remember her wearing a hat, once. So long ago it might have been grey or brown, so time has melted the colours. I remember her lying there, the silence that had been the content of her days. I remember the budgie that never sang, only screeched, a poor asexual budgie without a mate although she was told it wasn't right. That was before the silence blossomed in her like a tumour, cast a net around her, became her halo, her aura, her amniotic sac, her oxygen tent, her penumbra. Protection.

Just as she had come, she was returning, as soft, as silent. In April, the cruellest month, the same time coming and going. She had not, she said once, even let out a cry when she was born; instead she had hung there suspended, quiet, while they rinsed away the vernix, and tapped her, then harder. Stillborn, so they thought. And tapped her harder still, and she wouldn't speak out, wouldn't protest; that first cry took her a long time. She might have been the baby who invented the slap she was so quiet.

Mary make me meek and mild. Take me as your little child. She used to almost sing her prayers, wanting to be forever humbler than the dust motes rising up from under the bed in the sun, the silent afternoons with the sea crying in the distance. She wanted to be as contained, as silent, as Sunday afternoons in the 1930s in her village in the time before saucy American soldiers and automobiles.

When she married *him*, she spoke with a firm voice for awhile. It was as if marriage freed her tongue. She said "I do," and affirmed something, and whatever it was, it gave her authority. In one afternoon, with the end of the war making everyone giddy, with a veil made from curtain lace, she became an adult. That day she looked her father in the eye for the first time. Gloves and flowers. Men in shiny-assed and ancient suits that nowhere shade between brown and black hung on her every word and wished her the best. She the bride, the once in a lifetime thing to be.

Authority on a summer day, a week before the feast of the Assumption. Authority came with the man, her glove in the crook of his arm, and later rested in her hold on the four children who bawled from the day they were born and couldn't be shut up with a dumbtit. In those middle years, noise bloomed around her as she stood among the begonias; the yard was full of it, the house always sounded like hurried footsteps. When she heard her own voice coming out of her, it was like the voice of someone else, her great Aunt Sara she had admired, her aunt Sylvia she couldn't stand.

Now which of them did she take after? Whose voice? Who's the boss around here. She learned to boss well, the man with his sun-browned neck, his uneducated hands, the children with their minds like little flints, and even the chickens and the sheep in the yard. Shoo, shoo.

Discovering her voice. Get in! Get along! Move! Quiet! You'd just better try! Not in my house. Not in my yard. Not in my time. Later, after television caught up with her, over my dead body.

That was all before the silence blossomed in her like a tumour, like a flower. Then when she spoke, her words left a residue, harsh and bitter like ashes, to fall on those around her. She never swept up then, never swept anything away, although she moved the dust and the ashes from place to place, although always the broom sang swoosh-swoosh over the endless field of beige linoleum, the kitchen, the dining room, from morning to evening and to morning again like a restless pendulum in the long sleepless nights, nothing ever really got accomplished.

Nothing then could ever be kept clean enough. In the world full of filth, in the grimy Vale of Tears. They got a new radio. The radio on, the radio took over for her, and each song was about bitterness. And then the television, and from one o'clock until five o'clock, all the stories were about betrayal. She called them "my stories," although what the handsome young doctor in his white coat cheating on his languorous, blonde wife had to do with her was anyone's guess.

There were awful threats. Insomnia, silence, the blooms of tension among the geraniums, everyone else's fears. When she came to spend the long hours between the doctor's visits, I tried to get her to piece it all together, the words, her history, but she looked at me and in her grey eyes I saw how foolish I was, always looking for words to say it when there were none that mattered a damn.

"Who are you?" she asked me once, not remembering that I was the one who cried the loudest. She sat on the edge of the antique daybed and squinted out into the room, projecting into the middle distance what I had told her, trying to piece me together and probably coming up with Great-Aunt Sara. Or Aunt Syl, for all I knew. What was I, in pieces, a puzzle, a book for fine tuning the television translated from Japanese so that no one could pick head nor tail of it. How was it that I could drink tea, have crumbs on my mouth from the floppy jam-jams, all travelling so liquidly through the esophagus, through the endless complicated viaducts of the guts; how could I when I was in pieces? In order to help her, I'd have to be as round and hard as an apple. But I was too worn out from it all. I don't think she ever really recognized me again, me crumbling and falling apart on the chair.

Sometimes individual words fell out of her mouth and hung in the air; in bad need of a joke, I used to call them Random Islands. This was usually between meals; she needed her nutrition badly, and she took her food as if it were imperative that she not starve now. How many meals a day, nobody knows. In her silence she was remembering the Great Depression. No sugar, no butter—once, near the end of the month, no flour even. Bugs in the old brown flour sent out by the government. Six cents a day. The cow drying up, like all the females, attrition in her dry tired body. Once, raisins. They had eaten duff with raisins for a week. Stuffed themselves. Once pork. Crying over the slaughtered pig, eating it with their eyes red over the plates. No more where that came from. Everything final.

Then she would eat the endless slices of lemon cake and stare at the ceiling. The cow, finally driven mad from eating hallucinogenic grasses, had jumped over the cliff. Waves washed its body, pickling it whole in the moonlight.

Between the doctor's visits. "My head is full of the queerest things—you wouldn't believe it. I can't say."

"I have to go to work now," I would say.

"Listen!"

What she wanted. An electric dryer. A trip, I don't know—somewhere. To leave once and come back and turn the key in the lock and go in and make the neighbours lust for her account of it. To pay off the stove bought on instalments. High leather boots that didn't pinch her calves. To hold her head high. A house with children in it to visit. No heartburn. A frost-free refrigerator.

When she mumbled, half asleep from medications, I used to ask, "What did you say?" and she'd give me a black look. But her words spread out as if melted, dripping around the sharp edges of things in the tidy house, so organized, the silence constructed so well with its mitred corners, its cabinets and drawers with their liner paper and balls of camphor.

The TB. She hadn't gotten it, but a big crowd did. Sometimes everyone around her was coughing. There wasn't a glass fit to drink from. The germs lived everywhere, in coat pockets and barn rafters and chimneys and tin dippers left by the sides of wells. In closets, in drawers, among your best blankets, blankets not needed anymore, blankets pulled over heads, faces, big ones, small ones. Too many gone, the house next door shut up, its trapped germs barred up to live forever. Don't go near it. Survivor's guilt, like memory, like a nightmare could come back on you anytime.

Like a lot of women, she found that when she had something to say, someone always interrupted her. Snotty children, growing fat and lippy on education, feigning superiority that the parents themselves encouraged only to get slapped in the face with it. And the man of the house—*him*—sitting on a kitchen chair pulling his boots off and snipping off her long sentences with his cold eyes and his pocketknife, making a little whistle out of wood, whittling away as if he had all the time in the world. Or him sitting there barefoot waiting for her to pick up the cue that *he had no socks on and where were they*? She going on about pinch-pleated drapes and sickness and letters from her sister Paula who was married—away—to a stationary engineer, and who had everything.

He would suck in a long breath through a gap in his teeth and cut her off just like that. It's no wonder what she said sometimes sounded childish, monosyllabic, and full of bits and pieces.

She had a habit of saying, "What?" You could be in the parlour sitting down and talking among yourselves, and she'd walk in with the broom or the mop dangling from her hand as if it lived there, and she would lean on the door frame and say, "What?" And everything would go silent. You didn't know where to pick up, what to fill in, what she had already heard. There would be a quizzical look on her brow, and you wouldn't know how to respond. She wanted to be a part of all the conversations that happened around her, and she would walk away offended. Someone was always hurting her.

Him. He was the one, I suppose, who hurt her the most. He would go through the trouble of cutting her off, leaving her sentences hanging in mid-air, all to utter something short and crackly, like static, of his own. Like the battery going in the radio just as the announcer yelled, "He shoots, he..," there was always the loss of the unsaid thing, a frustration that something else should have occurred, some breakthrough or climax. Such impotence. In them both, their surroundings, the things they made with their hands, in the fruitless children travelling in endless circles around the globe fooling themselves that they were trying to do good, were looking for something better. Such stillness. Out of the rocky soil, the thin earth.

In my place. She couldn't adjust, the place so sterile even I could hardly negotiate it without feeling like an interloper. Not a cooking smell ghost to linger in the cupboard, nothing that needed to be thrown out. In that place, the shiny and unused kitchen of a single woman, middle-aged, who ate out all the time. Who never had need of an orange peel baking in the oven to mask the cabbage. No smells, no wonder she got lost on the second floor and stood all day in the window, facing the alley where nothing ever happened, unable, it seemed, to turn around. She tried to find her way, tried to put a mark on the place. Date squares, cut glass squares, jelly roll, lemon dough-nuts, all melding in the pale grey carpet, hitherto untouched.

Her prayers. Spilling, like her head, over the end of the couch, the words dripping out into the night. Awake, asleep, you couldn't tell sometimes except for the dribbling words. The Magnificat. The Sorrowful Mysteries. One night, falling off the end of the Glory Be to the Father, "Take your hands off me!"

I brought tea, and drank it until my kidneys floated away and I was left light-headed. "If I had my time back, I'd be like you, I wouldn't have no one." she said.

In this room now, the silence, the dust. I can hardly believe the sheer amount of it; what was she, a myth of a housekeeper? What irony: me rejecting everything about her and becoming more her than she was, me with the place where not a mote was

left to write itself in the sunlit air when the window was open.
Me developing an allergy to dust, finding it now hard to tidy up,
suffering like a martyr, the unmarried daughter with her mod-
ern, idiosyncratic diseases left to shake out the old coats and pile
the old shoes in musty boxes. Here, in the closet, dried flowers
she must have thought would make a potpourri. Not quite dried,
the dew too heavy and persistent, they are turning to violet
mildew in my hand. Why even throw things out? No one will
ever live here again.

I suppose in the end I should take it all to *him*. Him in the
nursing home, floating in and out of the transient world of the
Alzheimer's sufferer, him jumping on to every boat of an idea
that comes his way and jumping off again just as quickly. I could
take the boxes, now destined for the Salvation Army, down to
him and unfold her history piece by piece, the panorama of half
a century stored in clothing and bits and pieces, and tell him that
she is gone. Does he know? Who is it that he cuts off now from
long reminiscences? He had, she said once, in the end found his
own way of leaving her. I want to tell him now it's a game two
can play.

Yet all I feel is a queer, directionless sorrow, for her, for him,
for their mutual struggle, the legacy of hardness they gave me
falling away, me spilling over the edges where it girded me like a
belt, kept my figure and my mind intact, for all these years.
Falling open in this room—me of all people—only it is too late
to change a damn thing. I, too, am set in my ways, and the
mirror, the one she never looked in, tells me this. My mouth, its
straight line. My body, ramrod posture.

Sometimes, I look in the mirror in my bedroom now,
looking for signs of age. I am an ageing orphan, or nearly. This
is proof of age. Naked sometimes, I cup my breasts in my hands
and feel the loss of elasticity. I turn and see on my thighs the
finger indentations of time, the stuff euphemistically and dis-

gustingly called "cottage cheese." And I have to turn my head in certain ways to the sun for the light to make it young again, brilliant, the same colour as hers. Becoming her, finally, the fate of the child who has just buried a parent and will soon, inevitably as November, bury another.

What to do with the little cards, her exercise books saved from childhood, the scapulars and magazines and the Royal Reader with her name written proudly inside the cover? Leave them here? For it strikes me that someday this will be my house, and I could leave everything the way it is, a document to the dying century and forgotten stories. And yet I will never live here, will never sleep in this long, narrow room with its dust-furred mirror, not lie here where she slept with him and then dreamed herself off into oblivion alone.

It is simply too engulfed in her silence. Like the houses she told me about, the houses that were shut up after the TB carried away the children, this house will remained closed, its windows as dark and as unrevealing as shutters until the peonies on the curtains fade from the sun and the young children of the village will dare each other to go up and look in, scared and titillated that they might see the old woman's ghost sweeping or staring, looking out the window at them in silence, until the grass grows through the front steps and no one remembers who they were who lived here.

Blown

*I*n the waterfront cafeteria where I take Tyler for lunch, a woman is talking to her friend. I'm listening—eavesdropper, next-table spy—for anything interesting. A story to tell Arlette later. Husbands, separations, renovations, hysterectomies. A slant on the world different from the grey, rainy slant my newspaper serves up in yet another daily ration.

"Look," Tyler says, "Walrus."

He has stuck two fries up his nostrils, and is giving me the look that says, "Watch me." It's the look he gives his mom when he's up to something, but lately Arlette seems distracted. "Finish up," I say, "only for heaven's sakes don't eat those ones."

"It's only stuff from my body. Our bodies are clean, " Tyler says, some quote from Arlette, no doubt. She's gone into a phase lately where the body is clean, there's nothing wrong with it, it's your body, celebrate your body, some bits of pop psychology and elementary health science blended with the odd concoction of self-esteem and sexiness that has been making her giddy since the new boyfriend came along.

Tyler sucks noisily at his plastic drink cup, scrunches it up. As we leave, I notice on the newsstand outside a tabloid image of a great fiery hunk of something slamming into what appears to be a planetary mass. "Urgent message to Earth as comet slams Jupiter!" the caption reads. "Scientists say it's proof alien life forms exist."

My kind of scientists. I buy the tabloid. Inside there is a

picture of Arlette's sister, Lisette, now an infomercial star with her own line of cosmetics. She can renew your skin, your life. On television, Lisette from our little piece of suburbia has acquired an accent from *Gone with the Wind* with which she delivers promises of renewal. "Slough off that mask of age and fatigue that's hiding the real, vibrant you!" she tells Arlette and me late at night. Arlette likes to zap her on and off, something she could never do when Lisette was in the room, in the flesh.

Lisette lives via satellite, beamed to us through the skies after midnight. On the back steps, watching for some small leavings of the Perseid meteor shower, I imagine Lisette plunging through the heavens, her high heels descending like landing gear. Perhaps she'll plunk down right in Arlette's living room. I listen. All is quiet on her side of the duplex.

I had just found this place when I was shopping at the Sally Ann and I looked over a rack of nubby winter coats and met Arlette's eyes. She talked a blue streak once she got going. She said things were kind of up in the air, and she was shopping to take her mind off it. She was between places, she said, her and her little boy. "I've got a place to rent," I said without thinking. Half a duplex, newly painted in soft hues. "Want to see it?" Because I remembered her as the quiet girl who closed her eyes and sang when she swung in the park. And I didn't want another neighbour who screamed at her kids and beat the backs of their legs with wet towels.

Now I can't help wondering if it was a bad decision. Arlette screams at Tyler, has pulled his shorts down, hitting him on the bare buttocks, adding humiliation to injury, while I stood there and did nothing. Only once, I have told myself. She only did it that one time. If it ever happens again, I'll stop her. I'll interfere. So help me God.

Arlette asks me about every second day if I'll look after Tyler for an hour or two. I say yes, and Tyler and I go off to the park or the beach or the mall if it's raining. One of the malls has a sort of indoor playground that Tyler calls our spot because I'm the only one who takes him there. One part of me hates the noise, the jangle of primary colours. The other part has eyes only for Tyler tumbling in the coloured balls, his hair standing wild with static electricity. Small darts stick in my throat when I watch him.

Sometimes, we go back to the house at the time Arlette asked us to return, and she's not there, and off we go again, Tyler whining, "Where *is* she," not a question. Only a statement of what has already become routine. Arlette in the morning, pale pink suit, white high heels. Arlette loves those shiny vinyl shoes, wipes them with vaseline on a rag. "Mommy's going out looking for a job, honey," Arlette says. "One of these days, Tyler, I'm going to come home with a really good job." Except even Arlette knows that you don't go job-hunting wearing an ankle bracelet with Babe on it. The job's name is Leonard. He is sloughing the age and fatigue right off Arlette, and she can't resist.

This morning Tyler and I are driving down a side street, going nowhere. Tyler likes these streets with their patches of light, the linked fingers of trees overhead. He lies back in the reclined seat, closes his eyes, feels the shifts from light to shadow to light again, says "In the cave, outa the cave," as we drive at the creeping speed allowed in wealthy neighbourhoods with overhanging trees.

"Catch it, Bonnie!" he yells, suddenly, making me jump. A purple balloon, iridescent and trailing ribbons of green and pink, is ghost-walking on a level with the hood of the car. I reach out my arm through the open window to catch it as it drifts by, but it swirls upward, caught by a sudden breeze, and Tyler says, "Get it, Bonnie," like he's going to cry.

So I do a crazy thing. I pull the car in to the sidewalk, and rush off after the balloon. Running up the avenue, reaching for the string until I feel it in my fingers. It pulls upward, half-filled with helium. I jump and grab it, hold it tightly and bring it back triumphantly to Tyler.

There's a woman standing by the car. She is tapping her foot and chewing the top of her left index finger.

"I just saw him sitting here alone, and the car running and—"

"I only left him for a minute." I'm fuming. Something in the way she takes us in, top to toe, gauging our sneakers and haircuts, like we're some kind of bandits invading these quiet streets where children are always accompanied, raiding privateers from the downtown core, balloon pirates.

"He saw a balloon floating, he wanted it." I tuck myself into the car. "Here you go, Tyler." I turn to the woman. "It was in park," I say, "the handbrake was on."

Why do such things enrage me? Driving toward our neighbourhood, I am all red inside, red and raw, the wind gusting outside to match my mood. Gusts catch the trees and shake them furiously, ripping at branches, the giant splayed fingers of chestnut leaves slapping the windshield. Chip bags stuck in the windshield wipers, congealed drops of sooty mist. All things blowing, blown. And Arlette is not at home. The steps are littered with store flyers dislocated from the mailbox perch. "Let's get some cocoa and watch TV at my place," I say, and rub Tyler's back.

Tyler likes the talk shows best, a taste he developed when Arlette spent more afternoons at home. He turns them on when I'm not looking, hoping I'll forget I disapprove. But he always gets my attention with his questions. He can't suppress them.

"Bonnie, what's a cross dresser? Why does that woman in her underwear have a whip? Is she a lion tamer?"

Sometimes I tell him the people on TV are actors paid to act crazy. Or I tell him they're from the States where Aunt Lisette lives, so don't mind them. His eyes pop wide. He knows Aunt Lisette is pretty strange and has lots of money.

But I've put my veto on the talk shows. Even though I'm not his mother. Skipping channels, we eventually find something for kids. A fake Grandma in a skewed grey wig is telling a story about making apple pies. She stares at the kids out there at home as if trying to hypnotize them with her popping eyes, speaks in a voice she imagines Grandmas have. Tyler's real grandmother is a blonde waitress who likes Barbara Mandrell and the colour pink in all its variations. I wonder who invented this screen chimera of aging womanhood, and just who she's supposed to reassure. The key clicks in the lock next door. Tyler jumps. "Mommy!" In these joined houses you can hear everything.

In these joined houses you can hear everything. The duplex life is full of intimacies accidentally shared. The soft sigh of satisfaction as a woman descends into a hot bath. Her flesh sucking against the tub. The sharp uncorking of wine. The far-off muttering of a child's nightmares; the long, dead silence before footsteps go to answer them. Arlette laughing. Leonard zipping his pants. On the other side of the wall, I creep around, under a cover of silence, not wanting it to be blown. Not wanting Arlette to know the tunes I hum, or Leonard to hear the cans I open. Not wanting Tyler to hear the drawn breath of my listening.

I have come to love Tyler. There, I have said it. At first it was just the babysitting thing, playing at motherhood, driving Tyler through the neighbourhoods of the city, watching him doze in the leaf-filtered light. Then something happened by accident. It wasn't supposed to happen. Things were to be very simple for me. I had taken a vow of non-interference, promised to leave no scuff marks on the world. I would live off the money left from the sale of my parents' house and its excessive, opulent acreage that was now an entire subdivision. I was not going to have to mingle with co-workers, or tangle with a man. I said "I'll never have children" so plainly to myself and so often it sounded true. I'd witnessed enough intimacy, staying home, seeing my parents through their illnesses, their drawn-out deaths noisy and passionate as opera. I had found a quiet way of being.

Then I stopped the car by a pond one fine morning in June, with a hawk crying *ki-ki-ki* in the hills. Sat there with a bag of bread for the ducks and watched the wind come in the window and riffle Tyler's hair, which was a thousand colours suddenly and gleaming. Waited for him to wake, and felt a great dangerous thing. Swore silently to protect him. To watch over him. As if I hadn't already done enough of that.

In my dreams Arlette finds a job and ditches Leonard. I look after Tyler in the days, and worry less about him at night. It's a perfect world.

Arlette, to my knowledge, only beat Tyler once. That time in her kitchen after he swiped a boiling pot off the stove. With a magic wand. Hot water flew across the room; pasta slithered over the linoleum. Arlette and I froze, thinking he must be scalded. When Arlette realized he wasn't burnt, she hit him. Fear has to go somewhere, I thought, as I stood by, my knees rippling like water. Horrified, but doing nothing. Tyler screamed as if he would never stop. It's a sound I've heard at a distance, through windows up and down the street. Never this close before.

Lately the street has been undergoing a kind of transformation, or invasion. When I bought these joined houses, I must have been the youngest person here. Old people peeped from behind lace curtains, and rarely stirred during the winter. Ambulances came on drifting winter nights and took them away. Slowly, the houses emptied; the curtains hung still.

The new people are young and vivid and noisy; maybe they were the ones who called for help when the comet slammed Jupiter. Jupiter seems like the sort of place they might have come from. Mostly, they are women with children. In the mornings, the women rub baby oil on their legs and lie on towels on back decks, catching the sun and yelling at the children. When the sun shifts position in late afternoon, they rotate to the other side of the houses, talking from one front step to the other about the temperature and the trouble with youngsters. All day long, the women holler at the children. They drink diet colas, beer or berry coolers, send the children to the store or to play on the sidewalk where they can keep an eye on them. Through the slow afternoons, Tyler and I swim in the pools of the city parks or lie on the back deck playing memory games and pick-up-sticks. Other times Tyler paints while I read. He paints wings in greens and yellows, purples and pinks, turquoise antennae, strange neon flying insects. My walls are covered with his creatures; when the wind stirs their wings, I imagine they will lift off.

It is Thursday. All week Arlette has been leaving in the mornings and returning at six o'clock in the evening. I make a mental note of this. Usually, when she comes home, there's a stir up and down the street. The women on the doorsteps push their hair back, cross their ankles, tighten the muscles in their thighs, push their sunglasses up or down. It's about Leonard, with his big smile that every woman feels is for her alone. If you can picture

Mel Gibson with a beergut, that's Leonard. And, hanging off his arm, in her pastel suit and pumps, Arlette dripping laughter. You might think she was a woman coming home from a day at the office. Except no one on the street has a job so no one thinks such things.

Rain batters the car, carries us chocolate bar wrappers and notices of pizza specials, plastering them against the windshield. I turn the wipers on high. Arlette is missing. And, travelling the streets of the city, I don't know what I expect to see. Her? Leonard's car? An ankle bracelet abandoned in the gutter? The last thing she told me: "You know what, Bonnie? You might just see a diamond ring on this finger someday soon." I froze, didn't want to think of Leonard raising Tyler. That was three days ago. I haven't seen either of them since. I tell Tyler that they must have gone off on a trip. I decide to take action, then pace and pace, wondering what action is and how to take it.

Tell someone. Make a phone call. But to whom? Social Services? Arlette's mother, Daphne? I called her the first night Arlette was gone. No, she hadn't been there. Daphne sounded tired. "She's just gone to a hotel with that Leonard. She's just taking advantage of you Bonnie, cause she knows you're there, and if you let her . . ." Contact the authorities. Tell them what? Arlette has disappeared but her son is all right with me. Yes, ma'am, we'll be right over to take him into custody.

Two a.m. Lisette is on television. I've got the sound turned down, but I can tell by her lips, her studied enunciation, what she is trying to tell me. To slough, buff, exfoliate, use this special cream with triple fruit acids, banish that fog hanging over you, honey, let your real self shine through. "Where is Arlette?" I whisper to the face on the television.

Lisette holds up her new hot-selling autobiography, as if offering me a clue. She mouths words I cannot hear. An 800-number flashes on the screen. If I call it, will she tell me where her sister is?

Two weeks. I have called Arlette's mother again. She hasn't seen her. "Should I be worried?" she asks. How could I possibly answer that. Then, "How's Tyler? You know you can bring him to stay with me." But I tell her Tyler's fine, I'll look after him. Between us is the knowledge, unspoken, that Arlette took off once before when Tyler was a year old and they were both living with Daphne. Arlette had been temping in an office and her boss had just gone through a bad divorce. He asked Arlette to go to Florida with him for a week and she went. I knew about this because she told me once that this trip had brought her out of the baby-blues she'd had ever since Tyler was born.

Still, this is different. The last time Arlette left, she told Daphne she was going. She stopped on her way to the airport to kiss Tyler good-bye. She phoned from Orlando to check on him.

As August passes, the world seems to become more insubstantial. Temporary. Some days I glance up and down the street, and the tenants of a house have changed since the last time I looked. A mother of two children is suddenly alone. Black rings frame her eyes. Another house empties one night. A week later, the occupants return, the woman, the three children I'd seen before, and an infant swaddled in the summer heat. I am beginning to believe in a world of silent, sudden changes, where people are moved from place to place in a second and no one witnesses it.

Tyler and I talk about Arlette in the evenings. We sit in his house or mine, and Tyler wonders out loud when she'll get back. I try to push the unpaid rent to the back of my mind. Tyler peers in the cupboards. "There's no Cheerios left," he says, "I wonder when Mom's going to buy some more."

"I'll buy you Cheerios, Tyler. I'm sure she'll be back soon."

He shakes the empty box. "I want her back now," he says.

One evening, when the TV ads are full of back-to-school specials, Tyler looks up from his drawing and says, "What about school, Bonnie?"

School. I don't even know when it's supposed to start. Fear sets in. Tyler is supposed to start school this year. But where? What school? After I put him to bed, I rifle the kitchen drawers, having seen Arlette poke pieces of paper in there. A letter from the Florida man, an apology about how he broke it off. A torn slip of an envelope with Lisette's address on it, which I take out, intending to contact her. Expired coupons for two-for-one pizza. Half a pink candle. Then, underneath, an envelope with the crest and letterhead of a school. Inside, the day and date, Tyler's assignment to a class, the names of his classmates, his teacher. A list of the supplies he needs. In spite of everything, I feel a little in control. Tomorrow I will take Tyler shopping for school supplies.

In the car, Tyler seems happier than he has for days. He insisted on putting the shopping bags by his feet instead of in the trunk. As we drive, he studies the bags, reaches in to take something out, turns the clean new things in his hands. Markers, crayons, a fat pad of construction paper. A red sweater with dinosaurs on it, small scissors, erasers. He turns these things over and over with a kind of wonder, as if arranging in his mind who this Tyler will be who uses such things.

On the radio, an announcer intones, "Police are seeking the public's assistance in the search for a sixteen-year-old girl.

Tamara Barnes is five feet, three inches tall, weighs approximately one hundred and ten pounds, and has short blonde hair. She was last seen yesterday in the Kenmount Road area wearing black jeans and a brown leather jacket . . ." Leather jacket. In this heat. She must have been planning to go far enough or long enough that the weather would change and she'd need that jacket. I realize I'm thinking in clues. I turn the radio off, but it's too late. I can feel Tyler's eyes burning a hole in my cheek. The heat from this makes tears well in my eyes, but I remain calm, "Tyler, love, I'm sure your mom will be home soon." My voice seems to come from far away, a thrown voice, not of my body coiled in pain around all its questions and doubts.

People, it seems, go missing all the time. You never think of this until it happens to someone you know. Then all reality shifts and new landscapes form, like the islands that rise from the sea after volcanic eruptions. You realize suddenly that many things you would not have believed have probably happened. And you yourself settle into a kind of holding pattern, a prolonged vigil for something that must occur. You walk past a newsstand and catch a headline that screams improbability: "Couple disappears from city street in broad daylight. Witnesses say they vanished into thin air." Suddenly this makes sense, becomes something you can believe, maybe even accept.

Locking the door, you notice for the first time the thinness of the lock, the hollowness of the door itself. You wonder why windows are made of something as breakable as glass. You think of ascensions into heaven, of the earth opening and swallowing people, vehicles. Or of spacecraft and alien abducting beams in the night. You begin to think that families are random collections of people that might change and reconstitute in different forms, without warning.

I put Tyler to sleep in his own bed, in that part of my house which is somewhere between rented and haunted. Barefoot, I search the rooms, telling myself I have the right. In the drawer where I found Tyler's kindergarten registration, I find a leather case containing Arlette's IDs. A thing I hadn't seen before; I wouldn't have looked in it. Only her driver's license is missing.

Upstairs, I stare at the clothes in her closet, trying to imagine what might be gone. The closet is nearly full. The only things that seem to be missing are the pink suit and the white shoes. On the floor, a pair of Leonard's jeans lie crumpled as if he'd just melted right out of them. Two of his t-shirts are on the dresser. I can't stop. I search every drawer, find only fresh socks and underwear. No telling absence or secreted missives. A lacquered Chinese box filled with costume jewellery and one real gold bracelet. Beneath the bed, boxes of sweaters and heavy socks, a few strewn magazines, a condom, a box labelled Xmas Stuff. I open it, and find an assortment of small, inexpensive toys bought on sale, Arlette getting ready early, knowing that December always finds her poor. Under the mattress a worn floral cosmetic bag. A roll of bills inside, twenties. Twelve hundred and sixty dollars. I sit on the bed with the roll of bills in my hand. A car cruises the street, slows, Garth Brooks spilling loud through the open windows. My heart bangs against the back of my throat. I stuff the money back in the case, shove the case under the mattress, hurry out of the room to more neutral territory. The car accelerates slightly, rolls down the hill. By the time I pull the living room curtains open, I can't make out its colour or make, only a dull red glow at the bottom of the street.

September is the opposite of March, yet has the same kind of drama. It comes in like a lamb and goes out like a lion, a sudden roaring gale one day tilting the year toward winter. But it always begins beautifully, my favourite month of new schoolbooks and fresh winds. Tonight a soft, moist breeze carries through the window scents of flowers from the park nearby.

We are in Arlette's side of the house. I stay here a lot with Tyler now, where he is surrounded by familiar things. But we use both houses; they have knitted into a single space, with rooms containing different pieces of our lives.

Tyler is sleeping. Tonight he cried briefly, and I held him and stroked his hair. When I do this, my body fills with a deep, warm ache. We talked about his mother. I was as open as I could be. I told him that I couldn't imagine that anything bad had happened to Arlette, although I really don't know for certain. I told him that every day I expect her to phone or simply turn her key and walk in the door. I can't tell him that this feeling has begun to ebb, that now I feel less sure.

I can't tell him there are things I can't do now—it's just too late. If I call the police, what will become of Tyler? And what kind of trouble will I be in for covering up her disappearance for three whole weeks?

Lying on the edge of Tyler's bed, listening to him breathe, I close my eyes and see an imaginary circle drawn around these joined houses. Inside the circle are all of these rooms, with their silent mementos and everyday charms against danger. Inside too is the safe, sleeping child, his breakfast waiting downstairs for morning to come. By the front door is a backpack stuffed with supplies for a boy's first day in kindergarten.

Outside, across the street, a man bangs his splayed hands on a door, "C'mon down Linda, Jeez, I know you're up there—we gotta talk." But what lies out there is of no account. Anchored and becalmed in this still, dark harbour, I lie and wonder how Tyler will feel tomorrow, and I rehearse mentally what needs to be done.

The morning will be bright with sunshine. We will eat

Cheerios in the kitchen and talk a bit more about school. We'll
go early and walk around, check out the playground. I will walk
Tyler up the steps to the school, hold his hand as we pass
through the plate glass doors. I will find his classroom, his name
tag. Whatever name the teacher calls me, I will have a noncom-
mittal way of answering. I have told myself that, whatever I do,
I will not lie.

The Incubus

*I*t was during the summer after I turned twelve, the summer that we arrived later than usual at the cabin at Mingling Pond to find the giant maple split in two and lying at the porch steps, it was that summer that my mother was visited by the incubus.

In the beginning, his presence was almost imperceptible. Black ash in milky white ashtrays. The brown stubs of unusual cigarettes. A rustling of fabric in the night. The screen door's bang! bursting into my sleep. Then silence followed by disturbed dreams in which laughter caromed around the walls and set them echoing. Then dawn but no rest.

My father had left in April. Every time I heard the screen door I would wake, leap up, heart pounding, thinking he had returned. Even now I hear his footsteps cross the rooms of my sleep. But I had heard his footsteps leave the house, and I never heard them return. The sound of an entrance is different from the sound of an exit. And often in sleep I still hear a woman's wild laughter.

This woman, the entertainer of the incubus, the beauteous Helen, survived to tell the tale of footsteps and laughter, but never did. She still lives, on that other coast across the continent. She has had three more children.

I do not see her. I have turned my back on the fog-wrapped

east, its cold that lies in bones waiting for winter to wake it, and I look to the Pacific, the blue-eyed sea, to save me from confusion. I will never go east again.

Never say never, Helen would say, if she still likes adages, one-liners, quips that say it all. Helen carried greeting cards in her head, one for every occasion.

I heard the creature on the stairs once. I was up with a towel under the door to block the light, since I didn't want Helen to come in and lounge on my bed and talk the way she liked to talk, a hand running through her wavy black hair, or a finger keeping time to invisible music against her knee.

I was reading about the witch trials in Salem, Massachusetts. Young girls like me turned to accusing horrors. Women with no explanations for dying cows and blighted crops, turned to dust. I was fascinated. Death was all around me, pulling me into odd books, movies about the occult, stories of macabre dealings between worlds, drawing me to tales of witches and to the possibility that the house, the garden, the street harboured secret, dark dimensions.

In April. It was just after Easter. I remember when because the house was still scented with the twin pungencies of chocolate and oranges, the leftover breaths of pastel mints and expiring lilies. I couldn't eat lamb that year, having gone off meat, not understanding two things: how anyone could slaughter lambs in the first place, and why no one objected to calling Christ the lamb of God, and then devouring his symbol in mint sauce. We should have adorned the lambs with ribbons and bells, paraded them through meadows braceleted with daffodils to the sound of pan pipes. I was queasy all year; even the animals moulded in chocolate stirred a deep disgust in me, even as their scent encouraged me to eat.

The beauteous Helen and the morose Patrick. Her with her skeins of wavy hair and him with the shuffle, the hands in pants pockets, the cuffs dragged down to sweep the floor. All winter they walked around each other, taking turns making patterns of concentric circles, dizzying arcs, moving in, close, then out. I would draw their movements with my Spirograph set. Obsessive patterns piled up in the study, maps to the house and ourselves and where we were in relation to each other.

Eventually, some time in spring, Helen and Patrick sat down, holding parts of their faces in their hands, the unknowable epicentre of something. The radio was playing country music, something about divorce and how this broken heart would not be healed by time. "Time wounds all heels," Helen said, and laughed.

"Turn off that crap, will you, Helen," said Patrick.

"You're closer to it. You turn it off. Don't worry. Good Catholics don't get divorced."

Even I knew he wanted her to change the station to show she was on his side. But, after a time, it was him who spun the black plastic knob in search of one of the three things he listened to—obscure news from far away, hockey games, string quartets.

One of these nights right after Easter when the air was soft with rain they were sitting there at the table when the tumblers in the cupboard exploded. We didn't know what was happening at first. A sudden profusion of bangs, glass popcorn, and a shivering of cupboard doors, a sparkly substance leaking out underneath. Small shards, tiny crystals stirring and settling like sugar, arrangement for glass and glass; the pieces were too small to whisk up, too lethal to vacuum. Helen mopped them up with cloths coated in Vaseline to make them stick. She said that she'd heard on the radio about a certain kind of glasses, imported from France, that were known to spontaneously explode on occasion. "And I heard on TV," she said, "that things have been known to explode or break in houses where there is a lot of tension. So I guess we'd better lighten up, folks."

The next morning Helen announced that my father was gone. She said it flatly, pouring orange juice into mugs and never meeting my eyes. And it was only later that I remembered hearing his footsteps, a sound filled with the eagerness and fear of escape.

During the summer, after I'd had my first period, Helen said I was old enough to know a few things. We'd just had THE TALK. She was sitting on my bed with a book in her hands. On the cover above a girl with an unblemished face, dressed in white right to her hairbow like a vision of an angel, were the words "Isn't It Wonderful to Be a Woman!" It wasn't even punctuated properly.

"Your father," Helen said, "has had some problems, dear. With depression. He told me about it after we were married, but he needn't have worried. I would have married him anyway. Things were pretty good back then. But, you know, it always took a lot out of him to keep up a face for the world." She hesitated. "You know those nights he'd sit out on the porch with a beer in his hand, just sit there for hours?"

"Yeah."

"And your Nan used to say, 'Look at Patrick, Helen. One beer takes him all night. You could have done a lot worse. There should be more sensible fellows like him around.' Well, what she didn't know was often by that time he'd have been at it all day. In some bar on the waterfront. Would have left for work but not gone to work. Would have been looking at the gulls and the boats and yakking with the alkies. They'd call me from the office."

"How can you say those things? He's not even here to stand up for himself."

"Look girl," she said sharply, "This is not the schoolyard and I'm not spreading gossip. What reason have I got to lie to you? And I'm not blaming him. I'm just saying that it was this depression thing. Everything bothered him, everything got him down, nothing could raise his spirits up and keep them there. And the beer seemed to take away some of the sadness. It's like there was always something ... missing ... in him. We can't blame ourselves that he's gone, Diane."

"He might come back."

"He might." She smiled, "How are the cramps? Did the aspirin help?"

"No," I lied, "I think I'll lie down." Just to make her go. She put the book on the night table, and the beribboned angel smiled through her period. Something missing in him. And in me. Missing him. Wanting him to come home so that he could sit in his favourite chair and sigh with the comfort of it and, after a while, he'd see me and say, "You're still my little girl." And I'd go to him and he'd hug me to the birds-eye check of his shirt until the pattern disappeared. "Always will be," he'd say.

But Helen didn't tell me what she knew about him until long after he was gone. When I was old enough. Early that summer, when the demon spread his black wings inside our house, I was not old enough to know.

Sometimes the incubus was hardly there at all. In my mother's room, I heard the pulling of chintz curtains, the wheeze of the wicker settee, whispers. A muffled conversation followed by a long groan. A sigh sometimes. But as the summer grew on, Helen's eyes bloomed inside dark rings, circling outward in search of something, darkening her whole face. Inside these smoky caves, opalescent gleams flickered and retreated, appraised and retired to secrecy. In her eyes you might find pirates' treasure. And then, in the evenings, she'd start to sparkle. She'd clean the house to an immaculate state. She'd wash the dishes and hold the new glasses up to the sun to check for spots. All the while, she'd be swinging her bum to the music on the radio and singing along. And as soon as it got dark, she'd send me to bed. Said a girl my age needed her rest. She had been lackadaisical in the past, but that was over. She had full responsibility for me now. I was not allowed to stay up and watch TV.

And so I could not talk to her about the demon, even as his visits became more frequent. I knew him though, by sound and by a name I'd found in a book last borrowed in 1947, by his throaty laugh and the sense of foreboding he left behind. Although I had not seen him, I had read about him. I had read about incubi and succubi, the demons of the night, male and female, knew how they could infect dreams and inhabit houses, lie upon the bodies of sleepers, leaving behind a little of hell when they left. In my borrowed books, I traced the lines of old woodcuts and shivered at the description, extracted from a woman by the Inquisition, of what an incubus did when he visited her. I held my breath and read of how the unclean spirit had been cast out. But I could not talk to Helen about any of this. Even as I saw her standing on the porch one night wearing only a peignoir. Stretching her arms toward the sky. A glass of dark red wine in her hand. I could sense him there in the shadows, outside my field of vision, watching her too. I could not talk to her. Even after he started bringing the things into the house.

The things, like whatever power had shattered the glasses, were capable of moving objects through the air, were able to shatter, cause disintegration. Invisible and winged, they were at my command, as if he put them there to tempt me, to take my mind off whatever else was going on in the house. I had only to lie in bed and let my thoughts wander, and things would move of their own accord. The air changed its dimensions, became a sky where things could move around and above me, where things could fly.

A book would shut, open, shut, open again on the same page. The cigarettes I'd begun to smoke would arrive on the night table, matches and ashtray following close behind. All this with nothing to set it going except the drawing of curtains at dusk and me banished to my room nursing queer pains in my stomach.

And the music box, given to me by the beauteous Helen and the shuffling Patrick, shattered to pieces against the wall behind the dresser. This smashed with so much violence that I was half afraid to pick it up. But I did after watching for a while to see if it would move on its own.

I bagged the broken china clowns with their pieces of smiles and put them aside. I would glue them, put them back together. The mechanism that had moved the music sat exposed, a metallic jumble, wires glinting in the scattered shards of moonlight that fell between the curtains and the wall.

It was natural for the incubus to get braver. What, after all, did he have to fear? The mother started to transform toward evening, became dreamy, perhaps influenced by some telepathic messages he was sending her. The daughter was in her room with a towel under her door to shield discovery of light and smoke, nursing a strange set of shooting pains centred in her lower abdomen, willing the objects in the room to stay still. I could sense that he knew I was in hiding. It was a captive house.

So he got braver. His footsteps grew more reckless on the stairs, and glasses clinked and jazz was turned up loud. I heard him laugh, a deep rumbling. He was enticing my mother, perhaps torturing her. Such sounds! Smothered laughter that was cut off suddenly. An abrupt intake of breath stirring the house with its urgency. A sigh like the end of a rain storm. Once, a frightening moan, sobbing, hoarse pleading, the words strangled, "Oh no, please." Only her voice usually; from him a deep silence, as if he didn't need to speak. Occasionally, a volcanic rumble you'd think was laughter if you didn't know better. I listened, let all my anger rise in me, and a doll rose off the dresser and came, arms outstretched, eyes locked to mine, into my arms.

The pigeons nesting in the eaves moved out. A heat, unseasonal in that city of foghorns and visiting silver tides of capelin that left the air rank, set in and occupied the rooms with a dusty fatigue. Strange insects appeared in the garden and feasted on nasturtium leaves. Dust motes lay unmoving in the glaring light. There were rumoured visits by ruby-throated hummingbirds. I kept pestering my mother to go to the cabin.

"We can't go yet," she said.

"Why?"

"Remember, I don't have a car anymore. Your father took the car when he left. Besides . . ."

"Besides what?"

"Well, Diane, we're running a little low on money. I'm going to have to try to get a job before the fall. Don't know doing what. But I promise, I'll get us up to the cabin sometime soon. Just give me a little time. I'll work something out."

And then one day when I'd just about given up, she asked me to be good and mind the house while she went out. About an hour later she came back and blew the horn of a bile-green station wagon. I was on the porch eating a tuna sandwich and reading about the habits of the undead when she showed up grinning from ear to ear.

"We got a car!" she announced. "We're going to Mingling Pond."

"Where d'you get it? I thought we had no money."

"We had enough for this," Helen said, tossing her black hair, "I drove a hard bargain."

A fury of packing. Helen said I wasn't packing enough shorts, and where was Maggie Jane, my favourite doll?

I said my legs were too fat for shorts and I was too old for dolls. I left out the news that Maggie Jane had flown through the night into my arms, her lapis eyes full of understanding. "Since when?" Helen said to both statements, but she sat wearily on the bed. "Diane, honey," she said, "this is a hard age you're going through, a hard age for a girl. But it'll pass. Believe me, it will pass."

"Any news from dad?"

"No, I told you I'd tell you right away if there was. I would, you know."

It was funny on the highway that evening. My hope all summer had been that we'd get away from the city, from the house, and whatever had invaded us would let us go. I knew that demons and spirits can follow you wherever you go, but Mingling Pond had always seemed a charmed place, and I felt the bad things wouldn't follow us there. In the car, I could feel a change coming, could sense the absence of any kind of *thing* that might come between Helen and myself, could sense some lightness stirring in the air. We had the radio on and Helen was singing, even as the sky went black, and fat drops came and sat on the windshield, heavy as oil, even as the wind picked up and carried sheets of water toward us like tidal waves coming out of the sky. The worse the weather became the harder Helen drove, her hands taut on the steering wheel, eyes focused directly ahead. By this time, the wipers did little but clear one onslaught to make way for another, and there were moments when I thought that we must have gone into a river and were slowly sinking. But Helen said, "sinking isn't a slow thing, honey, have a nap and I'll wake you when we get there," and there was something about her sheer determination, how she never even glanced at me when she spoke, that inspired confidence. Eventually, I did go to sleep, although I was quick to deny it later.

We arrived at the cabin at sunset, but the storm had gotten there before us, and it must have been far worse than anything we'd experienced on the highway. In a yard littered with flattened meadowsweet and blown roof shingles, the old maple that had been there long before Patrick bought the place (for a song, he said) lay prostrate at the cabin door. It had split and fallen, uprooting itself completely from the soaked earth. Its roots filled the driveway, its matted leafy head lay almost on the doorstep of piled, cemented stones. It looked sadder than almost anything I'd ever seen.

I was crying, for the tree, for the mess of the place, for everything being spoiled. "What are we going to do?" I wailed.

Helen opened the trunk of the car and lifted out a picnic basket. "It's not blocking the door," she said. "We'll walk around it. We'll deal with it in the morning. We'll have help later."

"What help?"

"We're going to have a visitor. If he hasn't gone off the road in the rain. It's a surprise. I'm not saying another word until he gets here. Come help me unpack."

HE. Her eyes were full of dark lights.

We didn't have to wait long. He came in a late-model beige car, and he wore clothes so new I could tell that he didn't spend a lot of time around woods or ponds. Creased chinos and low leather boots. A shirt of birds-eye check that sent shock waves through my heart. He had dark hair like Helen's, only carefully cut, and he laughed almost all the time when he spoke.

"This," Helen said, "is Mark Philbin. Mark, this is my daughter, Diane."

Helen put an arm around each of us and marched us inside. She filled their glasses with dark red wine, and even put some in a glass and brought it over to me where I was sitting on the loveseat, unable to take my eyes off the curly black hair emerging from the open neck of Mark Philbin's shirt.

I learned a lot that night, and the wine helped. I learned that Mark Philbin had his own car dealership, and that it was doing really well. I learned that he liked wine and kissing my mother every time she came within kissing distance. I learned that Helen had already told him a lot about me, although where she'd met him, and when they'd been together, I couldn't get straight in my head. I learned that Helen liked smoked salmon, which Mark had brought on ice just for her. I learned, as the three of us smoked, and Helen never batted an eye when I lit up, that she wasn't going to get a job in the fall after all. It would be better for me if she didn't. And I learned that my mother was going to marry Mark Philbin.

This is the way the world ends, I used to sing to myself, watching the sky for signs of catastrophe. Or at least the way it changes forever. Three months after THE TALK, when the unstated thing was that Patrick might return to make claims on me but never on her, Helen and Mark got married in an office during the Friday evening rush-hour. I never did find out how she'd found Patrick, how she'd got a divorce, and I'd never ask, and Helen was never one to volunteer information.

Mark insisted we move to a larger house, and when we did, I cleared out all my toys and gave them to the children's hospital. Even Maggie Jane, whom I'd loved, but couldn't bear to look at now after she'd come to me, her arms outstretched, sailing on nothing but air.

I had to give Mark credit for one thing. It was his presence that banished the incubus, or at least I thought it did. In the new house it was hard to know. Mark and Helen chose the largest room at the end of the long upstairs hallway, and they suggested I take the one at the other end, which had its own bathroom. But whatever happened, whether the spirits had stayed in the old house or whether Mark's presence kept them off, they never returned. Things in my room stayed where I put them. I slept long, dreamless sleeps. I heard no tortured moans, no long sighs, no breaths that occupied all the air until there was none left to breathe. And the period had already come, like long-awaited rain, banishing the pain and the deep heaviness in my gut, washing me out, leaving me lightened.

I suffered them. There was something wrong with it all, all that going out to dinner and exchanging secret glances. Helen and Mark quit smoking and said I had to too. And the beauteous Helen getting pregnant one time after another, three babies whom I loved, although I could not love their parents. Her still nursing and pregnant again. Always, it seemed, larger and more beautiful, building in size and force like a storm cloud. She who used to say to young couples, friends of ours, "If you want to have a baby, have ONE." I stuck it out, babysat and got good grades and ate coq au vin with them by candlelight, until I was seventeen.

Patrick committed suicide. Patrick found a medication that allowed him to function. Patrick still watched gulls from bar windows and was in danger of losing his job. These were the stories possible for Patrick, and I wanted desperately to know how he was. I had received four cards, three gifts, and one long, rambling letter asking for forgiveness since the night the glasses shattered.

Eventually I found him. I was on my way west then, and I found him in Calgary. It's funny about telephone directories, the secret lives they give up so readily. There he was. The fourth P. Donnell I tried. The others had all been women.

It was strange finding him in a city driven by oil and male bravado. Among so many large and loud young men seeking a fortune, my small, quiet father seemed like some shore bird blown in by a storm, what the birding books call occasional visitors. He was working in accounting, as he always had, and he had found help for his depression, but he said that drugs were one thing, life was another. The best thing was that he was on an even keel most of the time.

We were walking toward the rusty block of brick buildings that housed his apartment. I'd been surprised that it was a two-bedroom, as if he were always waiting for a guest. And I realized when I entered the room that I was the first person who had slept there since he rented it.

"Look," he said. "I did want to get in touch many times. I don't know what stopped me. I suppose I didn't know what to say. There were those scattered cards. I realized after a while that it was probably worse for you. A card, a gift: you expect something else. Some kind of follow-up. I didn't know I could deliver it. So I stopped."

He stopped short of telling me I was still his little girl, but he did ask me if I would stay for a while. But I'd become unused to Patrick's drooping moroseness. Now I discovered it dragged me down even more than I was already. I'd had some uncomfortable dark periods for quite a while. When we walked, our shadows were twins. Heads hung low, shoulders hunched, hands destroying the seams of our pockets. We were almost the same size. We both had a habit of saying, "Well, then, that's that."

"I'm on my way west," I told him, when he asked about my plans. "I'm going to find a job, a place by the sea. I'm going to grow things in a garden and listen to the sea all night."

"It's really rainy out there now," he said.

"I know," I said. "I don't mind rain."

"Well, then," he said, "that's that."

I suppose I have a lot of Patrick in me. It's what my friend Beth used to call my "grey raincoat." She said that usually I was wearing it but it was always a pleasant surprise when I wasn't.

One time when we'd talked ourselves all the way back through adolescence, I told Beth about that weird summer when I was twelve. It was difficult to talk about, but Beth drew me out. She'd told me so much about herself, and she said that she was dying to know why I always referred to my mother, father and stepfather as The Beauteous Helen, The Morose Patrick, and The Dashing Mark.

We'd just treated ourselves to champagne and oysters because it had been raining for six days in a row, and I had been thinking that I might like to try and make love to Beth, since I had failed with as many men as there'd been rainy days, although I used to be good with men. Besides, I could talk to Beth like no one else.

So I told her about how the glasses exploded, my father left, an incubus came to visit my mother and sent spirits to my room, and how at the end of it all, a handsome stranger had shown up and I'd lost both my father and mother.

Beth was quiet for a long time. "You know what really happened, though. Right?"

I was silent.

"Right?" she repeated.

I had nothing to say.

"Look, Diane, you were pretty suggestible at that time. There must have been all kinds of confusion in you. The things in your room—these things happen—puberty is a weird time, and some kids—"

"Beth, you asked me if I know what really happened. Of course I do. What happens is what you experience. And you can only experience a thing once."

The end of the day by the sea is a fine thing. Waves wash blue to grey, and there is no diminishing of beauty, only a soft change. The sound of the water stills me. Sometimes I make fires and light the sky with red.

They have written to ask me to please come to their twentieth anniversary. The card has a picture of them, now after the last child has left home, awaiting some kind of grand reunion. In the picture, they are in their garden, surrounded by the lacework of leaves, their heads together, black wavy hair melting into strands of its own kind, until it is impossible to tell where one head leaves off and another begins. I touch their faces. They do not seem to age, grow lines, go grey. But I do. I think of what Patrick said about giving a little, and then having someone expect more. I could put "I can't deliver" on the response card and mail it back.

This is a good night to light a beach fire. Rain threatens, and will put it out later. I fold the card inside an empty wine bottle, watch it stain red, insert the cork. I toss the bottle into the western sea. Such things have been known to travel great distances, arrive in the hands of strangers.

Until the Point of Departure

*P*hil opens the driver's door and blinks. Rime glistens on his eyelashes. "What *are* you doing, Anne?"

I'm sitting in the passenger seat writing in my notebook on the pages following the grocery list with its items checked red like corrections. I have the overhead light on—something Phil disapproves of—as if I'm sucking all the power out of the car, draining the battery with this small shaft of light that falls on the page, my hand and its pen, the smoke of the cigarette rising from the ashtray.

"I'm writing that it's Christmas Eve in parking lots all over the world. Merry Christmas."

"Well, not all over the world, is it? I mean it's only Christmas Eve for Christians. Or Christians who're interested."

"Yeah, sure. Maybe. But there's something in the air. Hey, aren't you glad the shopping's finally done?"

"Well, you could have helped with the bags instead of sitting here writing love notes to the season."

"Yeah, but you didn't help with the other shopping, Phil. All those malls."

I turn off the light, pocket the pen and notebook, butt the cigarette. Small closures. He waits for the car to heat up, turns on the wipers useless against the freezing rain. A fan of slush forms so that it seems like we're peering out from behind that frosted glass people put in bathroom windows. We turn around slowly in the emptying parking lot of one of the two supermarkets in the city that stay open until ten o'clock on Christmas Eve. Across four lanes, we can see the same emptying begin in another lot. We beat the traffic to the main street. The competitors will be counting the spoils; the cashiers will finally go home to assemble bikes, stuff stockings, place batteries in the lower backs of dolls that walk and eat and talk and burp and who knows what else.

With the coloured lights blurred, hopeful and desperate everywhere strung out on dead trees in wet front yards, I am full of sadness and joy. The wishing mood. I wish I were young enough to love Christmas or too old to care. Bottles are rattling under my seat where we hid the liquor from thieves before entering the supermarket. In that parking lot one night last week, a woman had all of her Christmas shopping stolen. She cried on the radio talk show, and donations poured in from listeners until she had more than she'd begun with. I interviewed her for the paper, treading a fine line because she didn't want her children to know their Christmas gifts were from regular people, not Santa Claus. It took me all night to write the story, Phil saying, "Jeez, it's a good thing we don't have children; how would we figure out which lies to tell them?"

"Silver thaw," I say to him now.

"Mmm."

"Silver thaw on the trees. Glitter storm. Look. That's what we called it when I was a kid."

He can't look, he says; he's trying not to have an accident. "Don't go distracting me with your lovely dialect." The roads are treacherous with black ice. He says I'm not helping.

Home, we unpack the eighteen bags that contain what earlier seemed to be pressing needs. Three kinds of bread. Smoked salmon. Clementines. Toilet paper and one more roll of gift wrap, just in case. I open a bottle of scotch and we stare at the tree and make small adjustments to the arcs of suspended wooden beads to get them just right. I think of something Phil's mother once said about the perfect trees of childless people. What passes for Christmas carols these days reruns in an endless prerecorded cycle on the radio. Somebody got a hat for Christmas and it's too big. Somebody's going to drive all night to get to his baby.

At midnight, Phil and I stretch out by the tree and open the gifts we have given each other. He has given me a food processor, which I have wanted all year. I have given him a Swiss army knife, the kind with the utensils that allow you to have wine and beans in the woods, if you ever got lost and remembered to bring the wine and beans. Phil wouldn't stay in the woods long enough to get lost, but he's pleased anyway. Like me, he wants clever things. Over the food processor and the knife, our bodies meet and we kiss. Once the kiss was a beginning. We would lie by the tree and make love, the coloured lights dancing on our bodies. Now, there is just this leaning together, the smaller heat of shoulders and arms, the sleepiness of scotch.

On New Year's Eve, we are going to Steve and Jenny's. "Ill-advised," I say, "they got a kid, they'll be too pooped to party."

"Any port in a storm," he says, and raises his eyebrows. But there has been no storm, only days of long silences. I get dressed up, but he doesn't.

"How are you, Jen?"

"All right."

"You going to make it till midnight? That's some spread you've put on."

"Oh, there's nothing to cooking a ham. Just cross your

fingers Adam doesn't wake up. I told the guys to keep the music down, but just listen, will you. Anyway, I've told Steve: if the kid wakes up, you're going to be the one to go up and lie down with him. Last year I was asleep by ten o'clock. It's deadly."

"What's deadly, Jen?"

"Oh, going up lying down with the kid. I can never get up again."

"Oh."

"Well, you wouldn't know, would you, you wild, free thing." Jen pulls the strap on my dress and lets it snap back like she's a bad boy in grade six. "Your turn will come," she winks, "tick-tock, tick-tock, your biological clock lies in wait. Expect an ambush."

All night I watch people, a thing I've taken to lately. Phil says it's because I'm writing for "that damn rag." I watch eyes catch other eyes, shoulders turn to or away in elaborate dances. I observe legs stretch, wanting to entwine or kick; feet, so innocently tucked under coffee tables, flexing and stretching like hands, wanting to touch, stroke. The objects of desire are not as clear as they used to be back in the days before we were all with each other five years or more. When Jen had long hair and Steve had no job. When I had a real job and Phil had a fiancee who was not me. Then.

Now. We do make love after the party. He removes my beaded dress with great care and slowness, easing it off my body, the beads whispering as the dress folds in on itself. I fumble with his jeans and the tension in his upper thighs. Undressing is the sexiest thing we do, still not fully mastered after so many years of practice. After, when he is inside me, and my hands knead his back, tangle his hair, working on memory, I think of a pink sand beach where I am walking alone, waiting for someone. Under my feet, broken bits of coral press into my flesh, burrowing to find receptors of pain, of pleasure.

I don't see Steve and Jenny again until the end of February. On a night when the hills of the city are lethal with ice, we meet at a place which I call the Sad Poets' Bar because it is where assorted members of the arts community come with leather schoolbags full of grant applications and stories full of plans and disappointments. We come for happy hour and stay on; having saved our money on two-for-ones already, we are now on our way to getting guiltlessly drunk.

"How's Adam?"

"Oh, he's great. The toilet training is really coming along. He—" Jen laughs, "Hey, did you hear that—get a mother out for the first time in months, and what does she talk about—toilet training? Holy fuck, Anne, you don't want to hear about that."

I don't know what to say. Yes or no? Tell me about toilet training or spare me? We sit quietly for seconds, minutes, drinking our beer too fast. We don't look at each other.

"Where'd the guys go?" I say finally.

"They're up in the corner playing darts." She gives me kind of a hopeless look. "Fuck 'em," she says, "you and I can have a good time by ourselves."

Hey, Jen, remember when we first met, we had such good times, we used to laugh until dawn and nothing stopped us, we used to take off on weekends, remember, your parents' cabin, and the barbecue going in January, and how we met Steve and Phil, and what a time, and the things we used to talk about, and . . .

"You're mumbling," Jen says.

"Am I?"

"Yeah, you're going on— 'member the time, and all that."

There's a taco chip sitting on Jen's left breast; above it a little salsa bloodstain.

"You've been shot," I say, picking off the chip and pointing.

"Anne," she says, waving three fingers in front of my face as if to wake me from a trance. "Anne," she leans over, "this is serious. Guess what? I might as well tell you. I'm going to break up with him. I'm going to break up with Steve. I just can't stand it all anymore."

Phil and I have not made love for two months. I record this in my journal and for some reason I doodle flowers all around the margins of the page. This seems somehow wrong, shameful, embellishing such a bare and unfortunate fact, but I go on, creating stylized tulips, branched, feathered, parrot, plain. Perhaps this is just because it is May and tulips are everywhere.

When Phil comes home from work, stowing his trench and attache quietly in the porch like some awful secret he can't bring beyond the hall door, he wants to know how the work is coming. I'm supposed to be writing a tidy little piece on this elderly lady who, having lived alone for years in a house crowded with antiques, has now opened her doors, hung a shingle, turned her home into a shop. It is my job to make the reader love this act of transformation, but I keep thinking *so what*. The journal page with its ten bald words decorated with flowers is all I have, nothing to show him. An item unlike any other if it appeared in the paper, perhaps on the page with engagements and anniversaries. Would thousands of others rush to publish similar declarations?

Over the page I'm hiding like a schoolgirl who doesn't want her spelling words copied, I look helplessly at the slump of Phil's shoulders in front of the fridge. They are the shoulders of a man who has not made love for two months.

All winter we've been arguing half-heartedly over minor things. Can he use my hair dryer to thaw the pipes under the sink? If he burns it out, will he immediately replace it? Why won't he just go out now and buy a blow-torch, or whatever it is? Can we just call a plumber if I pay for it? And who drank the last beer?

I cook stir-fry with the windows open to the soft air, fog gathering in the garden like a breath around the tulips and daffodils. Although it is spring, my—our—favourite season, I feel sometimes that if I closed the doors and windows, blocked out the moving air, Phil and I would simply lie down together and not get up. What makes such tiredness? In our bones, in our fingers, in our stilled appetites. If I were to turn from the stove now and stroke his spine with my palm, would his shoulders lift and align like wings? But I couldn't if I wanted to. We lie down and sleep without connecting. Perhaps we have begun the end of ourselves. Perhaps this is the way the dinosaurs became extinct.

Jen is having a housewarming, although house is a large word for the place she's found since she and Steve broke up. I still can't get over it, buying a house and having a baby and all that, and then breaking up. Still, Jen's new place has hardwood floors and tall windows that flood the four rooms with light; she and Steve had lived in what real estate agents call a starter home, full of tiny rooms, bad drywall scars, aborted possibilities, and wall-to-wall carpet in innocuous grey. The windows now, the warm wood, the shortage of furniture, all work to create a moving light-play, like sun on water. There's a light like that in Jen's eyes.

I am envious. I want to seek her out, get her into a corner to talk, find out what the hell the secret is to looking alive like that. I want to pry out the drawbacks, the regrets. But she's sitting on a wooden bench with Adam on her lap, greeting her guests, and

I am suddenly aware that I am only one of them. I am not the guest of honour, the best friend, the solitary listener, the one who will always be told.

"Jen," I say later, after Adam is in bed, "how is it really?"

We're sitting on an old-fashioned daybed in front of the fireplace which Jen has lit against the fog pressing against the house, oozing into its old pores.

She gives me a strange look. "What do you mean, Anne, how is it? How does it seem? Appearances don't really deceive, you know. Things might just be as they seem to be."

Suddenly, she pinches me, hard, and I jump. "See, Anne, you felt that. You're awake. Just checking." She pokes my arm with her bony elbow. "Stop moping."

Much later, after enough wine to blur any precise idea of hours and minutes, the night gone, I notice that Phil has been talking to the same woman for a long time. I imagine that he will sleep with her, and what I feel is relief. She's got the kind of hair that swings when she moves, and her high breasts are almost under her chin inside a black t-shirt tucked into jeans. I watch their faces closely, searching for the nuances of sex waking up and taking notice. I'm not going to stop it, I swear, but I can't help watching. Something so conspiratorial about them until I catch his words.

"Plath," he says, "committed suicide. How can you blame anyone else for that? Why are feminists so into creating martyrs?"

The woman's face takes on a raw red glow. But Phil's driving drunk and doesn't see the stop light.

"Phil," I say, "I think we should probably go. The babysitter will be wanting to get home," pulling his hand, moving him away from her, into his coat, out the door.

"What the hell did you say that for?" he asks when we're outside. He is reeling a little. I catch his arm, steadying him. The fog of wine dissipates, leaving my head hollowly clear.

"I don't know, it just came out. Needed to have an excuse to go."

We walk in silence, our arms tangled. Our footsteps echo the way footsteps do when there is nothing else to listen to, the sound of desolation in any northeastern city on a foggy night.

"Is this what it's about?" he asks. "Is *this* what it's about? You want to have a baby? Is that it? Is that why it just came out?"

"A baby? No, I don't want to have a baby. It's not that. It ..."

"Don't say it just came out. Things don't just come out, okay. So you want to have a baby."

He removes his arm, slaps my back too hard, "Jesus, Anne, who would have ever, ever guessed."

We are walking toward the harbour, to what used to be a favourite spot, a small park where you can watch the harbour pilot's boat with its red and green lights making streamers in the water as it goes to meet the large ships. We sit on a ledge of stone amid scratchy junipers, and Phil breathes so rapidly and with such effort that I can't tell if he is crying or trying to control some terrible rage.

"We could have had a baby," he says finally, flatly, "if that's what you wanted."

I want to break up, I think, trying words I've borrowed like a hat from Jen, but I cannot say them, I want to break up, it's the best thing. I cannot say anything, this night has gotten beyond me, and I am wondering only if we will be able to get a taxi because I am too tired and too cold and too hollowed out to walk and it is far enough to home for Phil to say any number of unexpected things.

Under the street light, waiting for the solitary entrepreneur

staying out late to pick up fares from fools like us, I notice that
Phil is already using the past tense. Could have. Wanted. And I
know that there is nothing I have to say.

There is no need for a passionate split-up; at any rate, it is
too late for one. We would prefer a violent, sudden death, but
ours is to be slower, of natural causes. Slowly, through all this
spent and wasted time we are moving toward a place where we
will simply have different destinations.

One day he will simply leave work and drive to a different
house where I will not be waiting. I think it is likely that he will
get the car. There will be no passion, only a turning over of days
toward that particular season. The way calendar pages flip in old
movies to show the passage of time; a cliche can be an economi-
cal device. Until that point of departure, we are together for
nights like this, each one scarcer than the last. If we are lucky, we
might not even recognize the end when it comes.

It's funny how some nights you can see ahead into distances.
We hold hands tightly as the cab swings into our arc of light,
seeing ourselves awake some night, far from now. Lying con-
tented in new beds somewhere in this city. Or tossing, turning,
remembering how easily we were ripped off.

Caryatids

*J*illian cried so much on the phone that I told her, come over, come over. Yes, with the body. I had hardly made out the story, her voice on the phone so muffled, a voice from another dimension. The speaker phone an echo chamber for pain, making Jillian sound like a Greek chorus.

Now she gets out of the taxi. She pays the driver and returns to the back seat, lifts tenderly a small bundle wrapped in a baby blanket, mauve lambs gambolling against green and yellow clouds. Where did childless Jillian get such a thing?

Jillian had not noticed the cat was ill. She had been reading a report on the plight of women in developing countries. She was deep in the struggles of the women of Eritrea—such hardship, such effort, such determination. So much poverty, she said, the sheer weight of the work of their bodies pressing her into the chair in her study.

The cat, Artemis. I am suddenly aware of the drooping bundle in Jillian's arms. She extends her arms as if she is about to hand it to me, as if she has walked long and hard through mountain passes and valleys and must make an end to a difficult journey.

"No!" The alarm in my voice makes us both cringe. "Let's sit out on the deck. It's a nice day. I'll get us some coffee."

"Coffee," Jillian says, enunciating as if she has never heard the word before. "Coffee."

When I come out with the tray, Jillian has settled into one of the big yellow armchairs that I built last summer because I had enough money for wood, but not enough for labour. I built them from diagrams in a do-it-yourself manual, and they didn't come out quite right. Sturdy but slightly askew. For a second I see the slightly tilted chair, Jillian leaning, and the blanket slipping off the corpse. Sun shining through pale grey fur. One of those pictures that enters the eyes wide and whole, and returns as an afterimage, disturbing your peace.

"Now tell me what happened."

"A tumour," Jillian says slowly. "Huge. Her abdominal cavity was filled with blood. She must have been swelling up for days. I didn't notice it—how could I not notice it. I was reading, studying, thinking. Then she started to look strange—lethargic. She wouldn't eat yesterday, wouldn't even swallow water. I rushed her to the vet but it was too late. They had to put her down on the table."

Tears streak Jillian's face, opening up the old tear tracks, an erosion advancing where the flaking patches of skin dampen, grow irritated, peel. Always I think there's a smooth new Jillian underneath, waiting to come out, to be released by a heavy rain of tears.

"It's my fault."

"She probably would have—"

"No. It's my fault. Then they phoned. Wanted to know if I wanted them to cremate her. I said, 'what's that like?' They said, they cremate them all together." Jillian shuddered. "I couldn't take it. I freaked. I went and got her."

Jillian has dry tracts of skin on her arms, scaly patches. As she sits with her arms crossed around the cat, she scratches the dry parts, digs at her red wrists, her fingernails drawing drops of blood as if she is committing the world's slowest suicide. I want to say "stop" in a fairly authoritarian way, the way I do with children when they won't listen.

"Where?" Jillian says. Our eyes search the garden for a place to commit a body to the earth. Jillian wants the spot under a small Japanese maple, but I say quickly that I plan to grow miniature irises and anemone and other bulbs there, and I will have need to disturb the ground before the fall's out. I go on about division and soil amendment rapid-fire for about three minutes of eternity, until I notice that Jillian looks as if she is staring into the face of pure evil.

"There," I say, "Under that willow down in the back. I won't be digging there, won't disturb her. See how the branches fall. A nice place, peaceful . . ."

"Yeah, okay—where's your shovel?"

"Here, this one."

We walk to the end of the garden, and Jillian stabs the spade into the hard earth. The spade leaves a mark like a comma, but nothing moves.

"Jesus—you'll have to dig it. I can't. I haven't the strength. Jesus."

She slumps on the spade, her hair lank and wicking the wisps of late morning fog that the sun is burning off. The air is soft, a windless stillness.

Down under the willow, tucked among its roots, are bulbs too. Narcissi. The small, fragrant ones. But they are old and need replacing, and I cannot save the whole garden from Jillian's fragile mood. I take the spade from her hands and dig. The earth here is hard, compacted; small stones ring on steel. When I am down about six inches, I shatter the damp narcissi bulbs with the spade's edge and leave them scattered at the edge of the hole like cut vegetables. A bead of sweat drops into my right eye.

"How deep do I need to go?"

"Deeper," Jillian says, measuring the cat with her eyes. "I don't want her dug up."

I think of the horrors of frost heave and shudder. I think that now I will never have a dog, no matter how often the children ask. I think that I will never be able to sell this house and move without betraying Jillian.

"Lynn?"

"Hmmm?"

"We need something for a coffin. A box or something. I can't bear to put her down there like this."

I straighten and rub my hand up and down the hollow of my lower spine where an insistent ache has begun to throb. "What kind of box?"

"Anything, just find something, please."

In my house there are many kinds of boxes. Lacquered boxes from China, inlaid wood from India, many kinds. My husband brings them back from his travels and presents them to me. It is his way of helping a messy person become tidier, and I admire his tact and ingenuity. "This one's perfect for stationery," he says, or "Just the right size for your glazes," but not one is the right size for burying a cat. My gravedigger's hands leave smudges everywhere.

A wicker basket catches my eye.

"It's all I have, Jillian."

"It will have to do. Wicker," she says in an odd way, looking at the sky where the sun is now brightly shining.

I hold the lid of the basket while Jillian places Artemis inside. She folds the blanket tenderly. Artemis's head lolls a little. She could be a cat sleeping, one of those cats in baskets you see on cute calendars except for the pearly half-moon of dead eye visible under the lids. Jillian folds the blanket again, tenderly over the face. We are still for a minute, kneeling in the grass, and then Jillian whispers something and closes the lid, ties the green ribbon that holds it in place.

Jillian tosses the first clod of earth, and then sits back on her heels. "You'll have to forgive me for being so weak," she says. I lift the shovel, again and again and again. I pick six saffron calendula and lay them on the mound. Then something else needs to be done, but all I can think of is, *The Lord is my shepherd, I shall not want.* But some awful joke about herding cats bubbles up, and I bite my tongue.

The day Joe left Jillian she looked exactly the way she does now. Peeling and raw and vulnerable, the one surviving constant the way she seems to soak up the world's moisture and pain. She'd come over then, staggering in the door, her arms trailing books and papers. She wanted a place to stay.

"But he's gone, Jillian; the place is yours. He wants you to have it. And, you know, things might work out."

"No," she said with finality. "And I can't stay there. And I want to be the one to leave."

"But it's too late . . ." and I was already sorry for saying it. And would be for a long time.

She went then, refusing tea and wine and scotch and shortbread and the dozen other things I tried to ply her with. I picked up her trail of dropped papers and kept them for her. I cursed Joe silently for his resilience, for the way he thought things through and thought they could be over. When Jillian went through the credit card receipts among the papers he left behind, she realized he'd bought the air ticket to Australia two months before he said anything about leaving.

Now, as I escort my ex-sister-in-law to the taxi, I say what I said back then, "Call me anytime. Okay?"

Standing by the double glass doors to the deck, I wait for my children to come home from the after-school club. I have put

Gorecki's Miserere on the stereo. Worn out from digging, I sit in the old armchair that affords a full view of the garden, and indulge in some quiet mourning. For a number of forlorn and wraithlike things, faded photographs, wispy apparitions like the faces forming and dissolving in the fog that always winds itself around the trees at this time of day. I pick up the travel brochures that lie scattered on the floor. Randomly I open one to the Parthenon at sunset, those stone-blind caryatids holding up the sky with whatever heaviness must fill their heads. For thirteen years, I have been promising myself I will go back there, feel that sun on my back again, always *when the children are older . . . when . . .*

Some days, when my children come home, they stop and look at me quietly. I can feel their minds whirring about the contents of my secret life, the life I have when they are gone. I believe they think I don't do much of anything. Once my waiting flesh was enough.

Now I hear the key in the door and their footsteps hurrying to where they know they can find me most days.

"Large day, Mom?" Alice asks, all twelve-year-old attitude.

"Oh, yes. I had to dig a grave today. Had a funeral in the garden."

Alice bends over laughing, but the little ones, Ben and Cara, stare rapt and waiting. Eyes on skewers.

"Oh, yes," I say. "Aunt Jillian's cat, Artemis, died."

"The one that tore up all her furniture?" Alice asks.

"Yeah, that one. Jillian wanted her to have a proper burial, so she came over here. Anyway, I've got to get a start on supper. Got to get this dirt from under my nails first." My hands are encrusted. All three children are staring at me now, their mouths open.

"Out there," I say, pointing. "See the mound and the flowers. Go say a prayer for her if you like."

As I turn into the kitchen, I can sense their eyes, wide, younger than usual, fixed on the vivid bouquet of calendula against the dark, disturbed earth.

Renovations

*O*n a still afternoon, he lies with his back to me. Waking, I feel the slight radiation of heat from his skin. I close my eyes again, content to feel that heat, not really wanting or needing to see anything, to use another of the senses.

After a while, he mumbles into the pillow, "It's getting near time to go."

I don't say anything. No need. The full gold of the sun has shifted out of the window, the sun and the day travelling west. Almost every time we meet to talk and make love in this fog capital of the world, the sun is shining. We are too old to take this as any kind of omen.

The bedside clock is still, stilled months ago, but we have our watches, one on each side of the bed. I rouse myself to look at mine. Yes, Jesus, twenty minutes to three. Just time to dress, to let the May breeze blow away the scent of secrecy, just enough time to get to the school, the same school, to enter separately at east and west entrances to pick up our children.

Wednesday? he says, just that. The rest hangs silent in the air.

Yes. At noon.

Okay.

Not much later, when I am hurrying up the school steps to meet my children, I catch a glimpse of him going in the other door.

I know I look like a woman who is having an affair. I catch my reflection sometimes in the mirrored facades of downtown buildings, and what I see surprises even me. My scarf is always about to come off, carelessly loose, waiting for a squally strip-tease. My knapsack is always half-open, zippers undone, papers and books threatening to spill out. All my clothes look like they've been pulled on in a hurry. My friends say: what have you done? are you on a diet? working out? They say I'm looking like a spring chicken this particular spring.

Out in the sun and wind and rain, I drink every ray, every breeze, every drop.

The brilliant world settles when I go home. It's not the children; they have the same wild energy, but for different reasons. It's my house, my husband. Matt brings the world to a stop, will only let in what the house can safely contain. The bright colours stay outside behind new blinds, lead-free. The wind heels, moans longingly at double-glazed windows, but can't get in. Drops tap-dance on the perfectly sealed roof. Insulation silences the bass beat of the neighbours next door. The sun seems too exuberant for the new, smaller windows.

At the new kitchen work island, I help Matt unpack the groceries. We chop vegetables on two boards with two knives; it makes things go faster. "Easy on the cumin," he says, "you know what the kids are like." He assembles a tidy pile of the bills we will pay now, another of the ones we will pay later. His warm hand caresses the back of my neck as I stir the pot. In bed, he is a rock I lean against out of all weathers.

"I want to go play soccer!" Angela says, petulantly.

Her father looks at his watch. "Too late," he says, "It's a quarter after seven. You need a bath. Look at your knees."

She pouts. I am grateful to him for his good sense. One of us has to have it. I might run out with her, my sneakers beating the pavement to the park, might stay out under the stars, kicking a black and white ball under the moon. Or rise up and kick that silver ball clean out of the sky.

Wednesday. I take the packed lunch to the apartment. He is already there, always early. His eyes are dancing. We eat our lunches huddled together on a wooden lounger on the deck outside the bedroom. No one can see us. The deck has high planks and rails, the sun-warmed cedar smell heady, narcotic. We don't say much. In the bedroom, he unzips my jeans, slides them down. The wind from the open window swirls around my legs, recalls grassing with teenaged boys in some impossible past that just might be mine. I unbutton his shirt, my fingers counting his heartbeat through the cotton. His mouth is a salty Mediterranean of olives. His fingers under the edge of my underpants are cold as ice cubes, as if all his heat is trapped in an elaborate knot in the centre of him.

"We have plenty of time," I say, after we've made love.

"Just don't expect me to do that again, I'm not twenty anymore."

We lie side by side, our fingers loosely joined as if we are making a fervent collaborative wish.

"Tell me all the beautiful things you've seen today," I say.

"Pears in a store window," he says.

"Tulipa tarda," I say.

"A host of golden daffodils."

"A man and a child kneeling in the grass to look at an insect."

"A typeface that was so clear, it held the words lovingly."

"You, I say."

"Careful, now," he says, raising an eyebrow. "Don't get personal."

I laugh, rub his belly where a laugh is rising, a deep, undulating thing, movement as much as sound.

"There," he says. "Just leave your hand right there."

Sometimes, he brings me odd things. He finds a plant on one of his walks, and he wants me to tell him what it is. He comes across a beautiful book, and he brings it so that we can lie on the bed together and admire the pages. Sometimes, we take turns reading the words. Poetry, often, but the books could be about anything. Botany, antiques, architecture. Myth, birds or history. It's the way the book is made that counts.

Once, he even brought a cookbook, a particularly sensual cookbook filled with recipes for things people hardly eat anymore, venisons and suety riches. "Full of sauce," he said, using the word's old meaning, brazenness.

We read recipes aloud to each other, each of us picturing one of those meals together, perhaps on the deck of this very apartment on a summer evening rampant with breezes, herbed with the scent of cut grass. Four or five courses, the arrangement on the plate a sonnet or madrigal. Brazenness on our tongues. Our legs under the table.

"Why is a cookbook making you look so sad?" he said.

"Oh, I don't know." But I did.

He jostled me with his hip. "Do tell," he said, half-joking but ready to be serious if that's what was needed.

"It reminds me of being just married," I said.

"Cookbooks remind everyone of that. Or make them wish for someone to cook for."

"You?"

"It makes me think of ageing. No, don't look at me like that. I mean such books are full of promises of health and happiness. The happy home, and all. And it's not a lie, is it? It just doesn't keep well.

"Tell me about what's no longer happy in your home," he said.

I half did. And he half listened, lying on his stomach, his head on his arms, one eye cocked in my direction. After I'd finished, I realized what I said didn't sound very serious. Hardly an excuse to be doing this.

"I know what you're thinking. Let's go," he said.

Whatever gifts he brings, the books, the plants, he must take them away with him. Or I might take away a small flower and drop it somewhere as I walk.

On Wednesday night, I teach a writing class, a kind of therapeutic one. All women. All women recovering from some trauma, the one called life. From the cataclysmic moment of birth onward to now, a storm of traumas.

The woman whose turn it is to read tonight has written a story about an abandoned woman, a good woman. Her oaf of a husband has left her, and she is on the way to self-reclamation. I listen as the story builds towards redemption, epiphany. The story is well-written for a beginner, although necessarily over-wrought. It is the woman's own story.

I'm glad the class takes over the discussion after we've crossed the trench of silence that follows the reading. I don't have anything handy to say. The oaf and the home-wrecker don't profit from their middle-age meanderings; the good woman finds a better, independent life. This is just as likely to happen as anything else. But no more likely.

Just as likely, they may all go on to do the same things over again, or different things that will give them just as much trouble. They might expand the circle of trouble to include other people. It's been my experience that redemption is something we reach for, but don't get. A little grace, now, that's a different matter. . . . These are my personal notes on the story, but she can't have them.

I believe I say something about continuity in the middle section of the narrative. Hadn't I felt I was getting a little lost somewhere? Good, let's talk about that.

On Friday, I'm there and he doesn't come. I eat my salad and drink wine from the tiny bottle I brought, the air suddenly cold around me, the sun brash. I put my sweater on, wander about the apartment, feeling that I can't leave. Where is he? I tap my foot on the hardwood floor, an insistent, nagging sound. "Where were you?" I might yell if he came in the door now, oh, the sheer irony of it.

Strange, this place. How all winter it has become another kind of home, private the way home is not. The apartment of a mutual friend, a friend who is happy to know someone will look after the place, find the mess and report it if it's been robbed or ransacked. A kind and genial friend, who knows. He's in Florence, lucky bugger, a rare thing among my acquaintances, an artist with money.

"He does so well because his walls are so bare. He has no unnecessary attachments." A lover's observation.

I look around now and see for the first time how bare the place is. How it seems to exist on its own, float or drift, as if the world has retreated from it. Two pictures of his, only, and, in the bedroom on the white walls, a print of Matisse's *Red Room*, the soothing woman and her fruit, what he thinks of, perhaps, before he goes to sleep. Sparse furniture in dulled primary colours, softened red, mulled blue, washed yellow. A place that would always seem uninhabited unless lovers were to walk in the door, breathlessly, opening windows, talking, eating, throwing themselves on the bed in anticipation or exhaustion.

Where is he? It's over, I tell myself. He's come to his senses. But I sit and wait. I wait to leave at the usual time. I take the children to the park, the late tulips fully out now, sit under a tree and open myself to their colours and stripes while two daughters and a son romp with a wild bunch of children from their school. Two old women in heavy coats talk about arthritis. They compare the rigor in their hands, lifting them up to the light. My own hands seem to stiffen in proximity to this talk. I can see the rise of blue veins in my feet, the way the skin of my knees is hard and rough-looking. You can have your face lifted to the high heavens, but old knees fool no one. My husband's wife, twelve years married, her nails broken from digging in hard garden soil, her hair dyed, her house waiting, a desk collapsing under work that needs to be done.

"Do what you did last week, Mom," Danny says, running up, colliding with my knees.

"What?" I say, distracted, holding his warm hands.

"Hang upside down on the monkey bars!"

An image flashes by me like a yellow finch.

"I can't today," I say, "I've got a dress on."

But it isn't that. It isn't that at all. It's the word *unseemly*, an old, stiff word. One of the arthritic women had said it. "I told her in no uncertain terms: Daisy, at your age that's just unseemly."

I never sleep on the night before the full moon. My husband knows this, and pays no attention. He sleeps his deep sleeps while I wander the house like a trapped shade, dusting pictures and writing down things that come to me, drinking a brandy, pacing, looking out at the burgeoning moon, wishing: fill out that small rut in your side now, moon, so I can get some rest. It's the only time of the month I get any ironing done.

Each moon of the year has its own name and this one, coming the first week of June, is the Full Rose Moon, bringing the buds out hard on the shrub roses, igniting barbecues in back yards, beaming a shrillness into the voices of children as summer rises inside them.

A shrill sound now. Jesus. The phone at this hour. One ring and I grab it. My husband and I have, between us, three parents in nursing homes. "What's happened?" I blurt.

It is the first time he has called me at home. "Sorry," he says.

"Oh, it's you. I thought someone had taken a turn."

"Flu," he continues. "They've all got the flu. First of the summer bugs, I s'pose. Bad. I had to pick the kids up at school early."

"Oh," I say.

"Next Monday then? I probably won't be able to before."

"Yeah. Goodbye."

I hang up quickly, glancing around, my breath caught in my throat. Unfair to make the phone ring in this still house. At his house, only his whispered voice in a dark kitchen. And nobody would notice, drugged to sleep with flu medications, no doubt.

I start to feel a great sense of injustice, much bigger than the situation calls for. Suddenly, I am a vulnerable woman, a woman who can't sleep, target of the moon and a careless man. This careless man is just that—care-less. What does he care if he wakes up my whole household? If I have to make teary explanations in the middle of the night? If my husband must finally be told, if he leaves or—worse—opens the door for me, hands me my coat, and points a finger at the silvered night. My kids crying on the stairs, Mama, don't go. All the details of a horrid melodrama come to life, fill the room. *Unseemly.*

I do not sleep all night, but dream while still awake. I dream that he shows up and confronts us. Tells me I have to make a choice. Matt gives me a hard look and says, "You're free to go." His eyes shine red, trapped in a camera flash or a cheap horror movie. The children's eyes are red too. They sail away from me backwards, retreating into a thick darkness that sucks them upstairs. I fall off a cliff into unconsciousness but jolt awake. I have had an adulterer's version of the Old Hag.

How is it that a woman of the late twentieth century, a feminist, can tell things to a man in bed that she cannot say to her women friends? Can tell him of her longings, her deep fears. Can tell him how ordinary things move outside her grasp sometimes, without warning. These things she cannot say to the circle of women around the restaurant table now. She has known them for years, through their youths, the pairings off, the births of children, divorces and near-divorces.

Her talk with them is aware of slippage, the sneaky truth worming its way out. She thinks of everything going on beneath all their surfaces. What hides behind that careful lipstick? That meticulously told story? What barricades have been built against confessions, the possibility of gawping responses, suggestions for therapy, whole body movement, vacations, massage and acupuncture.

She feels so removed she fools herself into thinking she's an observer, so removed she thinks of herself in the third person.

Monday and Wednesday. Or Wednesday and Friday. Every week through the spring those afternoons together, and now school is closing. I actually consider putting my kids in day camp, part-time, so I can continue seeing him. The minute the thought crosses my mind, I know I've moved beyond the place where I always thought I would stop.

The last Wednesday I spend with him, I feel something break inside me as I lie next to him. Sleepy after making love in the trapped heat of the June afternoon, he lies with his body curled toward me. So small it seems he's gotten, it is hard for me to imagine him the man he is unfurled. His breath smells of green grapes, and his hair is damp. I comb it with my fingers to let the air dry it out. I think of him walking out onto the street, walking back to his store, going to meet his children, and I want all his secrets to be contained. I don't want anyone to meet his ragged gaze and know instantly he's letting things get out of control.

"So," he says slowly, "you've already decided. I understand. It's just not something you can do—pay for someone to care for your children so that you can come and make love with me. I can see you can't. It's just—not you, is it?" His arms tighten around my waist.

There really is nothing I can say. It would be foolish to promise options, to imagine the conniving that would allow us to meet at night, or to think of the faraway fall with its yellow leaves as a time when something broken in this deliberate way could be stitched back together.

"You could pretend you're taking diving lessons," he says.

"You could pretend you're studying Cantonese cooking."

I will not tell him that my hag-ridden falls have been replaced by a dream of despair in which I am starting out all over again in a tiny apartment in Missausauga without the children.

"Or you could—"

"Tell an elaborate lie. Except I'm no good at it. This is different. This time's my own. No one owns it. No one even asks me what I'm at."

And now it's run out, is what I think later, in the park with the children; my time has run out with the school year, and my children, running ahead of me across the grass, have recorded this passage of time in their bodies. Taller, bigger, they strain against last summer's clothes. Ellen says her shoes are killing her: when are we going to buy new ones? Wasn't it on Friday, wasn't that what I promised last week?

"Yeah, Friday." I say, thinking of the silent, empty bed, no one to admire Matisse's ruby variations, no one to imagine sitting in that empty chair with its rush seat and the promise of refreshing the tongue with peaches. I will be in the mall, buying sneakers.

When we get home, Matt is half-lying at the top of the stairs. I freeze. My breath catches in my throat, and then I notice the mess, the tools. He's not dead; he's tearing out the hall carpet.

"I couldn't stand it anymore. I had to get rid of it. I've been saying all year."

"Anything I can do?"

"Oh, just fire up the barbecue," he says, "take the chicken out of the marinade."

The phone rings after midnight on a night of waning moon when I have no trouble sleeping. Panicked, I rush downstairs to get it.

"Hello, you know you shouldn't—"

"Hello. Hello—is this Peggy? This is Matt's aunt, Hilda? It's Matt's mom. She's in the hospital. She fell over the stairs. Had a stroke."

When Matt gets back from the hospital, the first birds of dawn are singing in the rowan tree outside the window. He doesn't undress, just lies down. I stretch my arm across his chest, ask "What's the news?"

"She'll be all right, I think. Some bed rest. She's in good hands. But you know, I don't think she can go back there living alone. She tried to get down those stairs. Fell. Luckily, nothing's broken. She's very bruised though."

He clenches his eyes shut.

"So we'll have to find her a nursing home space too? When she's better."

"Yeah, I guess."

"What about the place where your father is?"

"Don't know. Would he even know her now?"

We lie listening to the birds. A coral streak comes in the window and paints a strip of wall.

"You know what I was thinking." He hesitates. "After I left the hospital, I walked around that pond on the grounds. And I was thinking—I know this is foolish—we could have her here. A few renovations on that playroom downstairs; you know the kids don't use it anymore—"

"Matt—"

"No, hold on, I know it isn't realistic. She'd still need some looking after. You've got your job in the mornings, you've got the things you do. I wouldn't expect you."

"I couldn't do it, Matt. I wasn't able to do it for my own parents. You know that. How could I—"

"Why'd you go downstairs?"

"What?"

"Earlier. When the phone rang."

"To answer it."

"Why didn't you answer it here?"

"I didn't want to disturb you. You were—"

I am cut off by a sound, too violent to be a sigh, a long outrush of breath.

"Peggy," he says, "Peggy." A fingernail strokes my cheek; his voice has a quality akin to pity. "Ah, Peggy, you're not much of a liar."

From Cloud Nine

You think that you would do something different with your life, that whatever mess you got in, you would not end up like me. You think that you are smarter, wiser, that after the first time, you'd get out. That you would not have let it get to the point of weapons.

You think these things in succession and repeatedly as you move about the house. You recite your brave and true thoughts like a mantra, a charm, as you wash dishes, do laundry, send faxes to meet the outside world. You say what you know, sure, confident. Of course you do. Even when my consciousness is elsewhere, I can see it on your face.

From here, your face, your house, the promontory where your house looks out over the sea, the mad, maudlin world you travel on are a spinning mass of images. I can call any of those images to me anytime.

Just like—that.

You say—you would not have done . . . what? You would have banished him. I would like to see you try. You would learn quickly that you don't need a gun to your head to get confused.

What would you say if I told you that, after a while, there in that house by the cliff where the sea roared and traffic bypassed us for the paved road, that I reached a point when I knew I'd never leave the way I came in. He might have carried me over the threshold, but another man would carry me out. Just the kind of thing he'd hate, another man having any part at all to play.

You would say, "I live just down the road."

I would reply, in words like a tourism ad, "A small distance is a great difference." I need not remind you that the differences, the way distances appear through different windows, have nothing to do with the absence or presence of pavement, opportunities for escape, or cars.

And here? I need not worry about how to get around here. Or about escape. I need not worry about the body, or what might be aimed at it, or how it may be attacked and forced to open, or turn upon itself. The body was an obsession, the word made flesh, the flesh made burden. But the body has gone now, its molecules dispersed. I am on my way to becoming pure light.

You would say, "Why didn't you get out when it started?" Forgetting that I did. That I left and he came after me and brought me back. He had the keys to the truck, the money in the bank, a grip on my arm and the children already inside watching television. Waiting for Mommy to get over her silly mood. And I could tell you how I stood by your house and rang the doorbell but you weren't there. It is hardly your fault that you were not there at that particular moment. But he was standing behind me, and he said, "Look, honey, come on home. The kids are there, come on, let's talk it over." The wind whistled against your empty windows, and I thought, *he's got the kids*, and I went.

Later he insisted we kiss and make up, and I lay there beside him, thinking of driving away fast in a stolen car, while he poured champagne for me and told me that when we were together like this, *the way it should be*, he was on cloud nine.

How is your kitchen, does it please you? With its new centre work island and its blue striped curtains billowing against your watery view like the sails of ships in a race. Your renovations over these past months have been the remaking of a world, the hammering out of your pain. How is the planet, so bright and dark from here, so knowable and beautiful and scarred, with its clearcut forests and oil slicks and harbours full of shit? I need not wander its scarred surface in search of green spaces. I can enter it, rock in the sweet arms of Gaia herself. You could say she is the mother I never had.

What trivializes everything to a certain degree is knowing that any life is only one of so many lived, and that the lives we spend housed in the flesh of animals and humans are only a small part of our totality. This knowledge is only opened up, realized, when the need for flesh is removed. This last stint of mine in the flesh—it had its purpose—it taught me that no matter how long you have lived, how much you know instinctively and intuitively, how subtle your knowledge is, wisdom is no defence when you have others to protect and your enemy has a gun.

Enemy?

I watch your eyes change as the word crosses your consciousness. You eyes are as expressive as the sky with its crossings of weather, its breaths of climates making patterns. Who is entering your room with the breeze and infecting your thoughts with words that make no sense in a world full of solutions to problems? Such a word with no solution. Enemy. Kill or be killed. How easily you recognize it as not a word of your own.

Quick, shut that window. A low pressure system, rising wind. Already the day is changing, clouds lay grey patches across the sea.

The first time I told the cops, you know what they said? They said, "I'm sorry, ma'am, but we can't do anything unless he actually does something."

I said, "But he did do something. I left, and he dragged me back."

"Dragged?" He had his notebook out.

"Yes, he found me and the kids, and he wasn't going to let us alone and he threatened us and he made us go back."

"You didn't have to go back, ma'am. A safe place could have been found."

"I thought I was safe. He found us. He threatened us. My friend we were staying with got scared. She kept checking the back seat of her car, the locks on the doors and windows."

"I'm sorry ma'am. You know we can't prosecute unless he commits a crime. You could get a restraining order."

"And who'll enforce it? Who'll be there when he shows up in a rage?"

The officer looked out over the water, as if the answer lay there somewhere, mapped out in the intersections of the criss-crossed paths of container ships.

"Look," I said, "Since there's nothing you can do, you'd better get out of here before he comes home."

What I was thinking as he drove away was, *if only life was a matter of procedure.* If only things happened in steps. But they don't. Something else is always going on while something else is going on. You open the back door to air out the house, and the wind slams shut the door in the front. Or an angry man finds you and tears out the phone on the way in, before he proceeds. He'd be a fool to wait until after.

I watch them, you know. I suppose that is why I keep breaking through. It's not a good idea to do it too much, to remain too close to the physical world. It only brings the weight of sorrow. But they are there, and I cannot help it, and you, Christine, my twin, I am only sorry that my spirit cannot pass through the house without touching you. Eventually, a voice in the air intimates, I will bring you more joy than sorrow.

I cannot help but go to Abby's room to watch her hair spread out upon her pillow, her small bare arms always struggling to surround something, a toy, a pillow, the blankets sliding off to reveal her legs, her beautiful pink feet. She makes me remember when I had hands and what simple wonders hands can do. And Kevin, bigger it seems every day now, the roughness going out of him. And I whisper to your thoughts Christine, be careful, he is the kind who doesn't bend easily and might break. Even his sleep is a rigidity that allows no compromise.

I had to come see them, you know. Over planes of moving light, I could feel their pulsing energy. And that last view I had of them, with eyes limited by what they had just seen, could not be the last.

This is what it was like. You know the official story. The stand-off had gone on the whole afternoon, and the tension kept getting worse. No one had known it was a "situation" until you called the police when he wouldn't let you in. The fool, setting everything in motion, barking through the door, "Get away, Christine, and mind your own business. I've got a gun." Your footsteps scattering the gravel were full of panic, and I knew what had to happen. The lights, the cars surrounding us, the neighbours leaving their houses, the sudden isolation and silence, him sweating in the recliner with the gun in his hand. He turned on a football game to make the silence go away.

You will never know really what it cost me to get him to open that door. Right until the end, I knew he didn't mean to harm the children. He never did. It was just that he didn't know where they fit in in this terrible thing between us. They were always just there, to be fed and played with and taken to school, and he would look at them as if trying to figure out what they were doing there. When he let me open the door, he was still trying to figure it out.

I saw everything at once. The huddled figures, the row of official vehicles. Beyond, the world was wild and huge and windswept. I saw every star in that wide black sky, saw each one distinctly for the first time, saw the rising moon red among torn clouds. Without looking, I knew that he had raised the gun, moved slightly to the right to be out of the way of the door. I kept my back turned, stayed behind the children, as solid a presence as I could make myself between the gun and that wild open air. I touched their backs, urged them forward, "Run, Abby! Run, Kevin! Run, my love," I shouted.

I remember Abby's sweater was halfway up her back, and I felt guilty for sending her on this most important run wearing something too small for her. Kevin wasn't wearing a jacket, and I shivered. Then arms caught them, swirled them beyond the circle of crouching men. I turned.

The trajectory of a bullet is a long slow thing. I remember the raised gun. I remember the second the bullet left it, its whistling tracery through the air. I knew. I didn't try to turn away or throw myself down on the floor, cringe or cry, knew it would be pointless. But it's a long slow wait. They say such moments last an eternity. It seemed that way, until I found out how large is eternity itself.

This is what it is like. You feel you are running, even though you are frozen in stillness. You feel the way the air has been pushed aside. You feel clocks tick all over the world. You feel the flesh sear, part. It doesn't really hurt. What the flesh knows is heat and surprise, that and how numbness spreads.

Then the white-lit place. Whirling and whirling. Myriad lights. Between the bullet's trajectory and the first glow of the light's embrace, I lived every moment of my entire life. Fears and terrors crossed me like thin bands of darkness drawn over

scenes of incredible beauty, each looked on with new eyes, my
children, days by the water, the births, you and I as children, a
ball game, rain, our own birth, Christine, and beyond it to
darkness and muffled heartbeat.

They say the spirit world has windows that the living may
sometimes look through. I don't know, but I do know that it
works the other way around, that the world of the earth and its
inhabitants is permeable, allowing a visitor so many points of
entry that one can travel freely, as long as one still desires it. I still
feel that desire, somewhat embodied, having a memory of limbs
and the work of hands, the feeling that amputees are said to have
about missing parts of the body, pain or desire where no flesh
exists to hold it. Sometimes I feel that I am spreading my arms,
or taking steps with my feet, but what moves is a shimmering
something, a phosphorescence almost, that glimmers less all the
time.

You would say, "She always let things go too far."

I would say that this light is what we dream of, yearn for, can
feel once or twice in a lifetime. I would say that this was how it
had to end. He wasn't the kind of man to commit a small crime
first and get caught for it, caged while I ran free.

You would say, "She couldn't take the necessary action."

I would say I made him let me open that door although he
didn't want to; the closed house suited him. I would say that
since that moment, I do not even know what I am, not flesh but
remembering it, not yet pure spirit, but yearning for it. A
mystery, something vaguely molecular, flickering energy, the
insinuator of a necessary tale told in hints and vague communi-
cations that leave you perturbed. Lately you have been thinking
about ghosts.

You would say, "She should have got away from him for the
sake of her children."

And didn't I in the only way possible? Once I let those

children out the door, I knew how it must end. He saw finally the end he wanted, the necessary warped conclusion of a relationship in which there was room only for one man, one woman, one will. He and I alone together. No more jealousy. Total possession. And he had to end it for us both. And the children are safe now with you, Christine. Safe as houses, as the expression goes. He will never go near them again.

You would say, "I don't know what to tell her children, how to explain it to them."

Stop fussing, Christine. I am on my way to becoming pure light. Tell them I am eternal. Tell them I am the sun on their shoulders, the wind in their hair.

Sweet Fruits of the Dead

*M*ondays were always washdays in this house, and old habits still live here, although their owners are gone. Up early, I strip the shelves of the hall closet bare, lifting with excessive gentleness the handmade things of my mother's girlhood—fancyworked bedspreads, pillowcases sprigged with violets, bureau cloths, a small tablecloth with a clock and cake announcing teatime, although we never had tea, only a mug-up.

Now everything into the wringer washer, haul down the handle and way she goes, churning as loud as the day we first got it. "It's so quiet," my mother'd said. She seemed happier than usual, charmed. My father was already hauling the old gasoline one out over the steps, grunting and biting down on the cigarette hanging from the corner of his mouth. That washer had travelled the kitchen on fat, shaky legs, its motor putt-putting like a skiff's, a washer with every intent of going out fishing.

That's what my grandfather said once, "No mind if my old skiff wears out; I'll just take that washer there."

Out of the suds, then into the rinse with blueing to soak in liquid moonlight. Now rinse again. Out to the line with the drooping basket, Mrs. Mary Peter calling to me, waving, "A great wash you got done. And done early. You're just like your mother, you know, her eyes, her hair." Mrs. Mary Peter stands there, arms folded like wings in her cardigan, the rhinestones in the corners of her cat-eye glasses winking in the sun, until I mutter, "Go away, now, ma'am. It's not right. My mother's not here anymore." And I blink Mrs. Mary right off the face of the earth.

She's not supposed to be here anyway, she's long dead.

Noreen is not supposed to be here either, but there she is. On the beach where I am looking for sand dollars while the sun dries my mother's handiwork. Pebbles and boulders, the margin of fine sand. Once I had walked here with my first boyfriend, had kissed him hard here and told him I was going away to school. He said I was off my head to leave a place like this. He spun me around as if I'd somehow missed the runner moon, the shredded clouds, the pewter and cobalt sea. He wasn't going anywhere. But three months later the fish plant closed down and he left. My mother told me in a letter, he went out west, where they were all going.

"Noreen—is that Noreen?"

"It's me, girl."

"Look at you, you haven't changed a bit."

"Oh, you're a wonderful liar, Debbie, always were."

"No really."

Noreen pats her stomach, "Not quite the same," she says. She touches her dark hair and winks, "But this is all natural, and I'm sure yours is too."

We push large rocks aside to make a softer place to sit.

"I haven't seen you in—how many years, Noreen?"

"Oh, years and years, I don't know. I was home a few times, not when you were here, though. I heard you didn't get out here much."

"No."

"And your mother and father are gone now, I was sorry to hear."

"Yeah, gone. Five years."

"What happened to them? Were they sick or something?"

"No, they just—left. Said they were tired of trying to keep

the place up. And the lights going out in the houses around them. All their own crowd dead or gone."

Noreen shakes her head, "Imagine just going—after your whole life."

We pick up stones, toss them at the water's edge. There doesn't seem to be much to say. "How long are you out for?" Noreen asks.

"A good part of the summer. What about you?"

"Only for the rest of the week."

"Why don't you come up tonight—for a game of cards?"

Noreen looks at me funny. "A game of cards in your house?"

"Sure," I laugh.

Noreen is chuckling. "Your mother'd have a fit. Remember how she wouldn't let anyone else's youngsters in the house?"

I remember. Noreen and Yvonne and Marie all coming to the door. "Can we come in and play with the dolls?" I'd ask. My mother would hand out slabs of bread and molasses as we stood on the step, catch my eye and give me a dark look. She'd look down at their dirty shoes. "No, girls," she'd say, "play is for outside. I just washed the floors."

Always, my mother had just washed the floors. Mary Beaton's mother who ran the shop we went to said my mother wore out more mops in a year than some slatternly women wore out in a lifetime. Under our sink, bottles and cans of cleaners strained at the cupboard door, gave out strong smells of chemical pine. She had one cleaner, Dettol, that hospitals used. All this was deployed in the war against germs, which were everywhere, and which could kill you, had, in fact, carried away many in the old days. The hands of little girls might carry anything into your house.

When Noreen comes up the gravel path, she is not alone. A young man and woman are with her. The man has a case of beer tucked under his arm. "This is my son, Gabe, and this is his girlfriend, Maura. You don't mind, do you?"

"Your son? Oh my, I didn't know he was all grown up. No, I don't mind at all. We can play partners."

"That's what I thought."

Noreen and I play 120s against Gabe and Maura. Not much of a challenge. They have their feet dancing on each other's legs under the table, and they keep looking deep into each other's eyes and reaching out to pat each other on the arms when they lose their bids. Noreen and I just laugh and tally up the scores.

Five games, and they've won only one—pure fluke—and Noreen slaps down the five, jack and ace of hearts and it's all over. We drain the last of the beer, and butt our cigarettes in the overflowing ashtray. "I'm pooped," Noreen says, "I want my bed."

"You're over the hill, Mom," Gabe says.

"He looks just like his father, wouldn't you say?" Noreen asks.

"His father?"

"Yes, Bill, you remember Bill—I went out with him in high school."

"Oh Bill, yes."

"He died last year, Bill."

"Oh, I'm sorry, Noreen."

"Leukaemia. He was only thirty-eight. He had it for a long time. Still, I didn't think I'd be a widow at this age."

Widow. I wake at night with the word at the root of my tongue, a gag. It comes unbidden, like the hag of my old dreams. The hag with her grey lank hair, hanks of it like wool and her eyes that are black right out to the rims, and her outstretched hands, her mouldering robe or shroud or housedress. A woman down at the heels for eternity, and bitter about it. At night, she'd come when I'd eaten a lot, was full and happy with fruit cocktail and strawberry ice cream in my stomach. She'd come near the bed, creeping so slowly you'd almost wish she'd hurry up. I'd make myself wake up but she would still be there. I would call to my mother and recite The Lord's Prayer but my tongue was mute and the air deaf. Closer and closer, a woman stiff as a plank tilting toward me. I'd try to move, but be pinned. Night after night she played out her variations. When I wasn't on my back, I'd be crossing the small bit of woods between my grandparents' house and ours. The clingy spruce would grab my sweater, and she'd step out. Ahead or behind me, reaching.

And I think of her now, alone in this house for the first time, although she is not the widow Noreen's word brought to life. The widow is Aunt Doris. When my Uncle Harvey died, Doris went into a spin. That year, the worst fishing season in living memory, Harvey dropped dead while storing his gear in preparation for going away to work in the iron ore mines. I still remember Doris and the five children lined up behind the coffin. It was a horse that brought the coffin up the hill to the graveyard, and halfway up it shat heavily. "Jesus Christ!" Doris roared out. "Is this what it all comes down to, is this it, God." She shook her fist at the sky. Vicious, she was.

"Your Doris, now," Mrs. Mary Peter said to my mother over the fence. "That's a state to be in. Making a living ghost of herself."

And I lay in the grass by the woodpile and listened, listened because it had to be true then, the stories we all heard. That Doris was putting on her wedding dress and veil at night, and taking out of the sateen wrapping in her trunk her dried wedding bouquet from eighteen years before. And marching up that hill to berate Harvey in his grave, slapping the bouquet down on the fresh dirt while she roared at him. People could tell because of the broken bits of lily and fern scattered in the clay. And it was said she always yelled the same things at him, about how he was a bastard, and what was she going to do with five children on a widow's pension.

"Things come back to you here." Noreen had said as we walked up from the beach. I lie awake and shiver, the old sheets stick and pull, my skin a rash of childish fears.

They brought Bill all the way back from Fort MacMurray to bury him here. Amazing, that clinging to home. There is his grave, over in this new part of the cemetery. The cemetery's epochs are written in stone, the spun-sugar markers of the first half of the century; the shiny dark granite ones of the second half.

We used to scare each other here when we were teenagers. Daring the dead. Coming up the lane at night, shushing each other, the wind in the spruce and var keening words that someone could always just make out—"Listen to that."

"What?"

"Listen."

We'd pause just outside the paling fence, shining white in the moonlight, careful to avoid stepping on the Unknown Seaman buried among the alders there. He'd washed up on shore in 1917, too roughly used by the sea to identify, and our great-grandparents had buried him outside consecrated ground, fearing he might be a Protestant and a blessing on him might anger the Catholic God, bringing disease and misery and a bad fishing season.

There, by the grave marked only by a tiny grey cross, we'd choose who would have to go in and walk the periphery, then cross dead-centre and say a prayer before coming out. When I did it, a plastic rose grabbed by sock and my ankle was bitten by a wire thorn. I'd fought the urge to run, keeping my eyes fixed on the gate post.

Now, as I visit my grandparents' graves, I see that out of all the wildflower seeds I scattered there years go, only the violas have been strong enough to survive. Alders encroach, and wiry junipers with their black-blue fruit, and blueberries.

I was sent to my room for a day once for picking such berries. I was ten, had been wandering the hills all day with my bucket, and it still wasn't full. I traipsed and traipsed but I couldn't find the good spots. I had begun to think I would have to face the shame of returning half empty or else scoop some of the fruit carefully out, lay down a nice padding of fine moss and replace the berries on top. "A grand lot of berries," people would say then when they met me on the road, "a fine picker, you are." My parents didn't like such deceptions.

It was then I saw a carpet of blue to the west side of the graveyard. Following the rich trail, I was inside and picking still before I froze, bent over, looking at the stone by my feet.

I backed away slowly.

"A grand lot of berries," my mother said. "Where'd you find them?"

"On the hill."

She turned from the washing machine and scooped a handful from the bucket. Something must have let go in me then, shiver or shudder—the knowledge perhaps of not a lie but an omission—and she caught it.

"Where?"

"Most of them I got around the meadows." I tried to sound nonchalant. "A few up by the graveyard."

"How close to it?"

"By the fence."

"Not inside."

"A couple just inside. Just. Only a few."

"Oh my God, you didn't. Oh God! You know you should never, never do that!"

The berries in her palm hit the floor, their sweet roundness dancing a little.

"Go to your room, now, and don't come down until after supper."

Before I left the room, I saw her open the door, pitch the bucket of berries violently across the yard as if it contained some awful contagion.

Contagion was exactly it. Although *plague* was the word my father used when he came to visit me that evening. Permitted to leave my room now, I refused to.

"Who knows what plague may sleep, and where?" he mused. "That's what's on your mother's mind. She's got a powerful fear of disease," my father said. "It carries over to a lot of things. It's why you can't go to some houses—like your buddy, Noreen's, say. The polio was there once. Your mom thinks everything stays where it was. Waiting."

We were both quiet for awhile. I could hear pots rattling in the sink downstairs; a powerful hunger washed over me. I had eaten nothing but berries since morning.

"The berries now," he went on, "you can't eat them because of where you found them. No matter how fat and juicy they look. You can't pick berries off the graveyard, no one does. Maybe it's just old beliefs. But it's different with your mother—it's like there's something in the berries, something from the graves, you know, it doesn't sound nice, does it?"

"Death, dad? Is that what your saying? She thinks death is in 'em? She thinks I brought home death to eat, is that it?"

He scrunched up his face like he was fighting with something going on behind it. He rubbed his forehead to quiet the thing. "I wouldn't go so far as that," he said, "but don't go giving her the creeps, playing on the fears in her mind, will you?"

I promised I wouldn't. But later, in those teenage years, when I went a bit Gothic, it was her fears I tried to tease out, her ghosts.

Noreen and I go to the beach again; this time we plan it. We make a fire and have hot dogs and beer and even roast marsh-mallows, although we are less inclined to eat them than we were twenty years ago.

"Remember how we'd all share a beer, sucking it through a straw to see if we'd get a buzz?" Noreen laughs. "And how much gum did you chew before you went home, Debbie. You were so afraid you'd be caught."

"I was always afraid I'd be caught doing something," I say. "And the queerest thing is now what I remember most is feeling safe."

"She wasn't as strict as she seemed, your mother." Noreen pauses. "Let me tell you something. Remember I was supposed to go to the trades school that fall you went away. And I didn't, I went out west. Well you know what the situation was—I was going to have Gabe. It was an awful shame then, wasn't it? And then I was the first one at our house to finish school. I was supposed to be different.

"I was down here crying my heart out, over on those rocks over there. It was evening, the tide getting high. Your mother was walking here like she always did, said she loved the sea it was so clean, made the air feel pure. So she comes up to me and catches me bawling my eyes out. She says, 'tell me what's wrong' in a really soft way, and I spilled my guts to her, told her everything.

"I said my life was ruined, and she sat down and argued with me that it wasn't. She said I was only seventeen, and a long time from now I might be able to look back and see it was a good life, not ruined at all."

"She said that?" I am astonished. I know she would never say such a thing to me.

"She did. And after when I got big, and was out west with Bill's sister—hiding out, you might say—and even when he came out and couldn't get a job first, I used to think about it, think about that long time from now. When we'd have our own house, good jobs. I can still hear her voice saying those words."

"Well, that's incredible, Noreen."

Noreen starts to shake. She's laughing now uncontrollably, with her whole body. "She said something else to me too. She said she knew I wasn't a bad girl. She said if I was a bad girl, I'd be thinking about having an abortion. Hiding it, and all. She said good girls take their punishment."

Now I'm laughing too. "That sounds more like her!" I lift my beer bottle through the sea-scoured air, to the sky with its dippers where my mother first told me heaven was, "Cheers, Mother," I laugh, "Glad to know you gave her a warning."

"Cheers, yes, cheers," Noreen echoes, lifting her bottle high.

We toast the sky as if my mother is among the pantheon of gods, and not merely in a senior citizens' apartment building two hundred miles from here.

When Noreen goes back to Fort MacMurray, I feel I have a kind of low-grade hangover that goes on for days. I'd drunk more beer and eaten more unhealthy things with her than I had in a long time.

I have to pack and go myself. A week more, and it will be September, and my job and my husband are there in the city, waiting, certain I will turn up. I said I'd think it through this summer, the baby thing, figure out if I was ready. Tick-tick, it's getting late to put it off any longer and it seems foolish to me now after meeting my classmate's son all grown up. But I am the only one of my parents' children to survive infancy, and some old memory of the grief of truncated beginnings lies like a hailstone, small and cold, near my heart.

I begin what I think of as my inspection. I go through the house and return things to the way they are when I'm not there. I put the religious pictures back in their places; I could not be alone here with the stalking eyes of virgins and martyrs, Pope Leo and the saviour himself. I drape afghans and antimacassars back over chairs, turn upside-down the wine glasses that have only ever been used by me.

I hang a little bag of camphor balls in the hall closet where my mother's newly blued linens give off a summery gleam. Sometimes I imagine them in use in the winter, snowy like the ghosts who might visit here around Christmas.

Before I leave I will visit the graves again, a century of family and old schoolfriends like Bill who felt an irresistible pull to the idea of home. I consider taking a berry bucket and dealing with the implications when I get there. The hills lately have been gleaming with green leaves, blueberries swelling like indigo grapes, the air fragrant with accidental wine.

NDEP

*I*rene has been in my night class now for six months. In the room with the wall of windows where the ever-present night shines in. The night deepens, darkens, becomes flecked with stars, the constellations shifting as we move through each task left that Irene must conquer. Lately, her task is to master the types of paragraph her textbook tells her she must before she can move on to other things—narrative, descriptive, expository, persuasive.

I am a newcomer in Irene's life. She has been at this for three years part-time, trying to weave her way through the unfinished business of her lost high school years. She often stops our discussion of whatever is at hand to remind me, tell me why she didn't finish her education the first time around. She lays the pen down and runs her fingers along the edge of a book, flips the pages. She says, "You just didn't, you know, in our house. Nobody did. You had to be out working at a job. No one thought to stay in school."

I don't like to ask Irene questions. Looming behind any questions there might be a story ready to rush out. It might be a story I might not want to know. It might be a maelstrom of details that would surround me and batter me with small sharp particles, the kind that leave their memory embedded in your skin forever.

"Irene," I'm saying, "Let's look at this latest paragraph together. I really like the way. . ."

Her eyes are on the wall of night beyond the window. Her white fingers, drumming. On one of them, two birthstones in a family ring, a larger garnet and smaller topaz—January and November—swirl around each other in a restless dance. "What?" she asks.

"I was saying I really like the way you wrote about that Christmas—you know when your daughter was small. I could almost smell the gingerbread. There's a lot of fine. . ."

But she is gone again. A minute later, as I wait, silent, useless, her narrative clasped in my fingers, she returns from the night outside and says, "Sorry, I'm not right here tonight. I can't concentrate."

I don't ask why. I have had to cut myself off from that access so freely given. Sometimes people regret later the secrets they tell you, resent you for knowing as if you pried them out. Then they cast their eyes downward and shut you out so you can't do your job. What is in Irene's story is enough—it is Irene's choice about what to say. There is a beautiful Christmas tree, gingerbread baking to make a house, a woman, a small girl. In a story world of their own, no one else around.

Vince is both the overall program coordinator and the math teacher. The former role is largely about making and keeping records, long lists of names, notations, start and finish dates, question marks, percentage points. Tonight he asks me to come up to the desk and sit with him and compare progress notes. It is always strange doing this, talking in low tones, while the subjects of our talk sit and struggle through algebra, research essays, the periodic table of elements.

"Irene," I say, when she comes up alphabetically, "she's got something on her mind, more so lately. She said she finds it hard to concentrate. So she's moving through the work slowly, although what she does is more than competent—it's good."

"Same here."

"Anything we can do?"

"Well, she doesn't say what it is that's on her mind. Something personal I think, rough situation at home, maybe? Don't know the details though. She might be . . . well . . . on medication."

"Oh."

"I suppose there's no point in pushing her."

"I don't see how we can."

"Well, then, let's just keep an eye on it. Moving right along now—Leo?"

On nights when storms beat the city with wind and snow, very few people show up for these classes. They wait, the radio on at suppertime and through the dishes, for news of cancellations. If no news comes, some look out the windows and see only a blind night wrapped in white powder, feel the tiredness settled in the lower back like a vestigial organ, think of the long walk to the bus stop, and the ride, and the long way back. Then they look at their children doing homework, or hear the drone of the TV in another room, and the comforts of life are brought home to them, and they decide not to go anyway.

I have to be there or I won't get paid. Unless there's an official cancellation. Tonight only three students have showed up—Jim, who has been coming here for years and who gets stuck on things for months at a time and who clings to the place as some kind of haven to get him unstuck, Yvonne who is rushing to finish her final courses and who wants to begin university next semester, and Irene, who always comes, no matter what the weather.

Irene has brought another "paragraph," but this one is much longer, several pages actually, a story with an indented first line. She works on math while I read what she has written and compose myself enough to discuss it with her. The story shakes me it's so personal, opening up Irene's life, the place about which I will ask no questions. What bothers me even more is that I've encouraged her to write what comes to mind, yet I'm the one who will have to bring her back to the curriculum, to the book that spells out what it is she is supposed to finish.

When I was sixteen. . . Irene has written

> . . . I was going out with a guy who worked with my father. My father thought he was the best kind of a fellow until I got pregnant and then he didn't have a good thing to say about him. My father one night he got drunk and he told Frank to get out of the house and after he pointed to my belly and said, 'And you, too, you better find another place to live when <u>that's</u> born. I'm not putting up with it. Your mother already raised a family.' My mother was crying, but she kept turned to the cupboards putting away dishes and wouldn't say anything. She never would say anything against him no matter what was on her mind. I only saw Frank once after. He came in the car to where I was working the next day said he had to go away. He said he couldn't go back to the garage with my father because my father was going to kill him. He said he'd go to Halifax and get a job and when he settled in he'd send me a ticket and I could come up there and have the baby. But I never heard from him again. So before I was seventeen years old I was in a small apartment on welfare cause I was sick the whole time and had to leave my job. And I missed my mother. Oh, she'd come, but not often because my father was mad at me. And then I had my precious baby girl and she was the best thing that ever happened to me. . .

I skirt the classroom. I talk to Yvonne about her upcoming university classes, her choice of courses. Jim is shaking his hands under the table, agitated, calling me over with the steady beat of his feet on the floor, and when I go to him, he blurts out, "Hey Carol! I think I just figured it out. Finally."

"What?"

"Square roots! I've been at them for months. I now how it works now."

"Well, I'm glad. Tell Vince. He'll be pleased." But Jim just gives me a funny look that means *what for?* Jim always talks about math with the English teacher, and about English with the math teacher. He won't talk about science with anyone, but reads his text again and again with open, prayerful lips.

When I finally get to Irene, I am still thinking about what to say. My husband Ron has said that I'm "emotionally awkward" in these situations, and I get myself in trouble because I don't know how to respond and then get in too deep. I'm supposed to help Irene get through these different types of paragraph—narrative, descriptive, expository, persuasive. And yet I know that whatever is happening in Irene's writing comes from another place altogether. From a room where a woman stood and put dishes in the cupboards and cried for the dissolution of her family. From Irene's father, implacable, perhaps not knowing how to be otherwise. Perhaps just drunk and going too far and not being able to say it later. From Irene herself, getting out of Frank's car one night, many years ago, watching the car disappear up the road with the moon and Halifax at its end.

"This is a very detailed story, Irene. And very . . . moving. You seem to be writing something that really wants to be written out."

"Yeah."

I wait.

"It's like, Carol, it's like once I start writing it down, it won't let up. It's like I got to keep going. Don't understand that other stuff though."

"What stuff?"

"You know—in the book." She opens the text, finds the chapter. "See here—narrative, descriptive, expository—whatever that is—and where's the other one, oh yeah, persuasive. I don't know what all that means."

"Just think NDEP like I said—remember? Just remember you have to write one of each. Would you like us to go through it again?"

"No, I don't mean that. I mean I don't know what it *means*. How these things are different. How you're supposed to separate things. I mean when you write, you just write, don't you, and all those things might be in it. Or they might not."

"Well—"

"And if you wanted to write like different things—like a what do you call it—descriptive paragraph—how would you keep a story from sneaking in and making it a narrative?"

"Well, I don't think you have to *separate* things. I think this is more about looking at different forms, purposes. Let's go over it again."

"Not tonight, okay. My head's killing me."

"Okay."

Ron says I shouldn't take the job home with me. Especially where it's only part-time, and there might not be "any future in it," as he puts it. He doesn't like it when I pace the floor, reading papers, but that's what I always do when I'm figuring something out. And we need the second income, especially if we're going to have children like we planned, and my feeling is that if you have a job you might as well throw yourself into it.

Irene and I, I think, will never fully come to terms with the differences between textbooks and life. Now she says she can't

choose a topic because the topic chooses her every time she tries
to write anything. Now, she says, she is writing more about her
daughter, about her growing up, about all the things they did
together. The way she says "did" makes me fear her daughter
might be dead. She hands me the narrative one March night and
I make myself read it—twelve cramped pages with no margins
or breaks—and as I try to discuss it with her I feel that I might
cry although everything I've been taught has pressed me never
to encourage or respond to sentimentality.

"Would you like to see her picture?" But before I can
answer, Irene has her wallet out. She opens the wallet and there
sitting on top of a small stack of plastic ID cards, is a young girl,
mid-teens, blonde, her hair falling over her shoulders, her grey
eyes laughing above her serious mouth. It is hard to make a
connection between Irene and that girl in the photograph.

"Isn't she beautiful?" Irene asks.

"Yes, she's beautiful."

"Beautiful by any standard under the sun. A man on the
street said that about her when she was small, and after it was
what I always thought when I looked at her. That she was as
good and beautiful as anything on this earth."

Irene hands me the wallet. I look and look into the girl's face.
I don't know when it is appropriate to hand the wallet back. So
it just stays in my hands while I look at the picture, waiting to
find something to say.

"Cathy. That's her name. But she's gone now. I lost her."

Irene's eyes fill with tears.

"What—" I start to ask but Irene has already snatched the
wallet from my hand, dumped wallet and books into her tote
bag, hauled on her coat and gone out the door. Across the room,
I can see Vince's eyebrows raised as if he knows I've walked
some place off limits, crossed a line about which I should know

better. His mouth forms a word, several syllables in the air. I think it's med-i-ca-tion.

I walk home after ten o'clock through a night missing any glimmer of light in the sky. The streets are practically deserted, as if people fear that the closed sky, with no reference points of light to indicate depth or distance, might be too close for comfort. Ron will be asleep already, most likely. I consider going to a cafe for coffee and cheesecake, or to a pub for a brandy. I might sit and read a page or two from the volume of Derek Walcott poems I've been carrying around in my bag for days. Such poems might dispel images of a beautiful young girl who is lost, gone.

I dream about Cathy. From Irene's story about a birthday party. Cathy is nine. It is just like Irene has written, the cake made in the shape of a teddy bear with candy features, Cathy's face when Irene hands her the large doll. Then Irene screams in the dream and at the head of the table, behind the cake, there is only the doll, grown impossibly large, blowing out the candles. Behind her the door to the street is swinging on its hinges. Cathy is lost, gone.

Irene never misses a class. I almost wish now, although such wishing is unfair, that she'd stay away for awhile and get some professional help, come back more ready to deal with the tasks at hand.

I keep hearing her words carried on breezes from other conversations. "Lost." "Gone." "Beautiful by any standard under the sun." I think about Cathy carried to class each night in the wallet in Irene's bag. About the weight of her silent presence reduced to this. About how I don't know whether she is dead or alive. But Irene is not writing now. She says she's got to put the English aside for awhile, and work on her geometry which she finds harder than anything.

In May, as the wall of darkness beyond the window advances later and later, and we are often working amid a flame of sunset, Irene says she's ready to attack writing again. "NDEP," she says, "narrative, descriptive, expository, persuasive—whatever. Let me have another crack at it." And soon she hands me another long passage.

I tried to do the best by Cathy. Until a woman has a baby she don't know what love is. And though I was only a girl when I had Cathy, she was my one treasure in life. I knew it was my job to do the best for her and always look after her. And I did. And things were very good. When Cathy was fifteen she got in with a hard crowd. It was mostly through a fellow she was hanging around with, although she knew I didn't like him. I knew he was bad news but she couldn't see that. Eyes full of stars and didn't I know what that was like! They were staying out late at night, drinking, driving around. I knew he was selling drugs because I seen him with a guy from a couple of streets down from us. This guy was a known pusher. Then Cathy started talking about quitting school and about how she had her rights to live her own life. I was worried. I contacted the Social Services and I tried to get them to move us to a different neighbourhood to get her away from that crowd. But it was no go. And I was in night school so I couldn't watch her every minute. And I didn't want to quit because what kind of example would that be for her? And then I came home one night and waited and waited and she never came home. It was morning before she came home and she was on something. I suppose that fellow was giving her drugs. And I wanted to kill him. And I told her she couldn't see him no more. Never. And we had a big

fight, a bigger fight than we'd ever had in our lives. And
Cathy said if she couldn't have her own life with me, she
was going off to Halifax to find her father. And the next
day she went off as usual like she was going to school but
that was the last I saw of her. She was gone, just gone. And
that was two years ago and my heart breaks with the
thoughts of what might have happened to her.

This time, I cannot help asking questions. Better to cross a
line than to dream of a monstrous doll blowing out birthday
candles, or to wake in the middle of the night and hear the wail
of a cat in heat and think it is a missing child crying outside the
window.
  "Did she go to Halifax?" I ask. "Did you ever find out?"
  "Oh, she went all right. I don't know how she got there. A
young girl with no money. I tracked Frank down through his
parents, although the last thing I wanted was to have to talk to
him. Yes, she went to Frank's. But I suppose she didn't get the
reception she wanted. He's married now with four children. I
wouldn't say the wife was too pleased."
  "And he never called to say she'd been there?"
  "He never called at all, did he? He said he tried to buy her a
plane ticket back. But she wouldn't go. Said she never wanted to
come back. But he might have said that just for spite."
  "Spite? Why?"
  "I don't know. Who knows? That's what he's like."
  Irene says all her efforts to find Cathy through official
channels came to nothing. Wherever Cathy went when she left
Frank's house, she didn't leave breadcrumbs, a path of white
pebbles to shine in the moonlight, or any other signs for those
to follow who might be tracking a girl in a city of half a million
people. A small city, really, until you think about how one lost
girl is like a crack in a sidewalk.

On a Tuesday in May, just before night school is due to close
for the year, Irene brings in a file folder. "Here," she says, "I've
done it. Now can I write that exam? Here," she hands me the
folder, "NDEP—one of each."

The narrative is the long account of her life Irene has been
writing all year. The descriptive paragraph is a full description of
Cathy, complete with a copy of that last photograph. The
paragraph is so detailed that, even without the photo, you could
see Cathy in your mind's eye standing right in front of you. Irene
says she will circulate the description and photo through
women's centres, youth facilities and social organizations. The
expository piece is a letter to the Social Services people and to
the Halifax police, updating them on her attempts to find her
daughter and asking for their further help in her search. The
persuasive piece is an ad, heartfelt and direct, promising no
recriminations. Irene will, she says, place this ad in every paper
in the country if she has to. She will find the money to do this,
she says, even if it means she doesn't eat.

"Well, what do you think?" Irene asks.

"Oh God, what can I say? Write the exam. Try to follow the
instructions closely. And good luck. I hope you find her."

I come out of the clinic in a kind of daze, struck suddenly by the
heat and sun after the air-conditioned, shadowy interior. Worse
still, I think my feelings are going to spill out, right here, right
now, in a public place. All year I've been trying to get pregnant,
and now it's happened again, another negative result. I exhibit
all the symptoms—missed periods, morning sickness, a sleepy,
heavy feeling, aversions to certain smells and tastes, and yet I get
these negative results. Every damn time.

For a second I catch a glimpse of the day before I seal my
eyes inward so they notice only necessities like the proximity of

traffic. In that second I see azure, white and gold, school colours, a day made of flying pennants, dandelions exploding out of every crack in the sidewalks. I try not to think the mean thoughts that clamour up from inside me, about how all those women and young girls who don't even want babies are having them every day, dropping them no trouble at all, while I can't even have one although I desire this more than anything in the world, just one—

"Carol . . . Carol . . . Hi!"

The bright voice is only a couple of feet from the sidewalk.

"Carol . . ."

It takes me a while to realize I'm the Carol being called. I turn and see Irene on a park bench in the grassy area outside the clinic. In her arms is a small child, perhaps less than a year old, asleep. The wind ruffles the child's hair and it rises in a pale wave that crests on Irene's cheek.

"Irene," I say, "hi . . . how are you?"

"I'm great."

"And what are you doing—babysitting?"

"This is Kayla. She's my granddaughter. I found her, Carol. I found Cathy. She saw one of my ads when she was looking for work. She was in Halifax still. On her own. She'd had this little one. I'm so glad I found them."

I look around, expecting the girl in the photograph to materialize.

"Oh, she's in there." Irene points to the clinic, its entrances marked psychiatric associates on one side of the building, family practice and maternity on the other. Her face darkens, full of a new sorrow with which she has just become acquainted.

"She had a rough time, Cathy did. I don't know what—everything that's happened to her—but she was in a terrible state when she called. Well, I got her home. She's seeing a specialist," Irene says, refusing the word "psychiatrist."

"That's great," I say, "that you found her. I'm so glad."

"I saw you coming out of the other door."

"Oh yes, one of those weird summer flu bugs, you know. Will you be back in school in September?"

"You know, I don't think I will. I think I have enough on my plate. I think Cathy's going to need some help for a while."

"Oh."

I am thinking of the time Irene handed me the wallet, how I didn't know when to hand it back. And of how this moment is like that other one, in that now I don't know when to leave, or how to. The baby in Irene's arms stirs and settles. Her hair makes me think of spun gold, words from fairy tales. The baby grabs Irene's thumb, holds it tightly so that her fingers blotch red and white, tries to pull it to her mouth, makes sucking noises.

"Oh, she's hungry. Hold her for a second, will you, while I get her bottle."

I hesitate and Irene notices. "Oh, don't worry," she says, "You won't give her the flu."

And before I know it the baby is in my arms. I feel the first aches of menstrual cramps buzz in my abdomen. I look at the waking face, the way it flutters into consciousness, the way the eyes register the sky, the spidery shadows of eyelashes across sun-washed cheeks.

"Thanks," Irene says, taking her out of my arms. "Isn't she beautiful?"

The Prime of Life

*I*t's the waiting I mind the most.

Although a lot of things seem to piss me off these days. Like the city councillors giving themselves free hockey tickets, and not doing anything about clearing the sidewalks. A person on foot simply has nowhere to walk. If I lived in the States, I'd slip and suffer trauma and sue their asses off. Then Joey could go to all the hockey games he wants.

This howling wind. Minus eighteen, and the proper dress for a job interview still involves pantyhose, my legs red where the wind blows the coat apart above my boots. My red knees at the interview, something harsh and a little too begging about that, a woman who doesn't have a car, can't afford a taxi. All of a sudden you can see in their eyes that they've thought of the damning word—"absenteeism"—with all its connoted blame for declining company profits, as if a few underpaid women missing buses or staying home with croupy youngsters was the real killer in this endlessly declining economy.

Still, I turn out a beautiful resume and suffer the red legs and smile. I want what they have to offer, even if my fantasies take me elsewhere. Through the stinging powder of fine, blown ice, I see the bus approaching, its whole side painted over with images of fast food. The wind grabs the wrinkled plastic bag containing my shoes and whips it out, like I'm carrying a bag of garbage or something. I can feel tears, stung out of me by the wait and the chill, melt through the cover stick under my eyes.

The bus is so warm I could ride it all day. I hope it goes way beyond the Village Mall, all the way to Florida.

At supper, I am fierce with Melanie. We are sitting at the kitchen table eating chili and rolls and Melanie is talking about how stupid her teachers are. She rolls her eyes to heaven and makes fun of them. Her voice goes gravelly, then high. Since at other times these teachers can do no wrong, I know she's hanging out with some boy who is not doing well in school. Fourteen and she falls in love about every two weeks, and she takes what these boys say to heart. She wants so badly for them to like her that she will agree with almost any opinion. When she gets interested in some guy who's doing really well, she's all for studying after school and talking about university. It irritates me, having to listen to all those borrowed opinions. She could have enough of her own if she bothered.

Now we are sulking over cookies for dessert. Both of us, but not Joey. Joey is the sun slanting over the ice, the charm of black-capped chickadees calling at the feeder. There is simply no sadness in Joey, and he doesn't mind me and Melanie much, sulks that we are.

"Can I have a sleepover?"

"Who?"

"Just me and Trevor and Cameron. Next weekend." he says, guessing my next question. "Please."

"Will I have to stand guard to make sure you don't break up the house?"

"Nah, Mom," he smiles, "We'll be good. We were the last time."

"The last time someone took my cigarettes."

"That was only Curt. And he won't be coming. He's gone to another school."

"Oh. Will I have to buy you all pizza?"

"Oh, would you?"

"I might."

"And rent a couple of movies?"

"Sure."

"I'll have to find something to do that night," Melanie says, huffily. "All you bratty kids making noise."

When she turns her back, Joey and I put our faces down in our arms and give each other a long slow smile. I reach my hand over and fluff out his light brown curls, watch the highlights catch fire. He doesn't like me to do it much these days, not when any other kids are around, but he'll let me do it when we're alone, and he'll let me do it for pizza.

When Joey was born, I held him close in my arms and swore that, this time, I wasn't giving up one bit of this child for a man. Not one bit, one tiny secret moment. I lay in bed with him, and Melanie, who was almost seven at the time, would come in and occupy the curve of my free arm. We hauled the TV into the bedroom because the living room in that house had drafts that lifted the carpet and flung the drapes against the sofa. Sometimes, when Boyd came home from his night courses, he would find us huddled together asleep, the TV on, the bed full. "You're turning into the great Earth Mother, Laura," he'd say at first, nuzzling my cheek and kissing the children. He'd try to find room, but we'd all be too sleepy to move, and he'd look at the bed, trying to find his place, and he'd smile and take the heavy spare bedding and go off to sleep in the cold living room that listed like a ship in the wind.

After a while he lost his patience with this arrangement.

"Whattya think?" Cheryl says, holding up a red crushed velvet dress that sweeps to her ankles.

"You planning to grow a few inches before the weekend?"

"Honest to God, Laura, I shouldn't go shopping with you. You never have a good thing to say. What about this one?"

She holds up a green one in the same fabric, only this one comes to about three inches down her thighs.

"More in proportion to your height," I say, "but a bit oversexed. What does he do for a living?"

"Computers."

"He'll love it. Go for it," I say, laughing.

Cheryl and I are up at the Pricebuster looking for bargains. The thing we love about liquidations is that the stuff could come from anywhere. You might find Grandmother's Ella's flannelette nightgown right next to some flimsy bit of a shocker from a Montreal boutique that hit on hard times. Sometimes we don't buy anything at all, just wander around, holding things up to our bodies and asking each other for opinions. We can use shopping for anything. I'll say "Cheryl, you'll look like a geriatric baby in that one," and it means I've got a bone to pick with her. She'll say "Laura, you look so thin in that," and it means she's forgiven me for something. That way we cover a lot of ground without getting mushy.

"Shouldn't you be home waiting by the phone, Laura?"

"Why?"

"What if they call?"

"I got an answering machine."

"Where, for Chrissakes?"

"At a flea market."

"Lah-ti-dah you are now!"

"Not if I got it at a flea market."

"Did you check it? Are you sure it works? I mean people are always trying to sell junk."

"Oh, it works all right. Anyway, I don't think they'll call."

"Why not?"

"I just got a feeling, that's all. I can see a form letter with my name on it."

"Only $19.99."

"What?"

"The dress. Only $19.99. What do you think?"

"If you like it, go for it."

"You getting anything?"

"No. I'm not in the mood. I can't afford it."

Usually, the day I get my UI cheque I feel pretty good. But there's only a month of UI left—five weeks to be exact. Every time I look at a price tag, I hear some old scold whispering in my ear *you're taking the food right out of your children's mouths.*

On Friday night, Cheryl brings over her youngest, Emma, and kisses her goodbye as she sprawls in my arms before rushing off to the restaurant to meet the computer guy. Cheryl's wearing the green dress, but has toned down the effect by wearing opaque stockings. She catches my glance, my smile. "My legs announced today they're thirty-eight and would like a bit of modesty," she says.

"That's fine," I say, "They go with the rest of you."

Emma's hair tickles my face as I cuddle her. We watch The Little Mermaid and eat Cheezies. Joey hovers on the sidelines, pretending he's too old to like this kind of movie.

"I don't like him." Emma says.

"Who?"

"Gerald."

"Oh, why not?"

"Mommy acts really foolish when he's around. She talks funny. I don't like him."

"Mommy never goes on dates," Joey says. His expression is a cross between admiration and pity.

I love the kind of relaxation the weekends bring, a letting go, a falling down. The phone didn't ring since Wednesday's interview, and they said they needed someone right away. So every day I'm sitting on the edge of my seat. But on the weekend there is no vital tension that something might happen. I can walk by the ringing phone without jumping, circle lazily, pick it up slowly. And then the immediacy returns on Monday, palpable, a lump in the throat: I must do something! Quick! Every time I open the cupboard doors and see the packs of compressed noodles, I know I can't face welfare. Not ever again. In a way, I don't want any of the jobs I've applied for. They're all office jobs and will require constricting clothes and hobbling heels and a certain respectful demeanour that I find hard to summon these days. Still, it's a bit late for choice.

But today it's Sunday. I can let my waist push comfortably against grey sweats, saunter around in flat boots edged in salt like margarita glasses. I am at the House of Assisi, my mother's next to last resting place. It sounds like an Italian couturier house except it's full of nubby cardigans and old slippers.

"What's she like today, Helen?"

"Not much change, girl. She's in and out you know. Yesterday she was as sharp as a tack. But today . . ."

I am always relieved when Helen Harris is here. I can feel this thing coming from her to me, a warm, practical reassurance, as real as her flesh, her footsteps, something which I can only describe as her humanity. My mother is sleeping, or somewhere, part of her face submerged under the pile of blankets she needs to keep warm, even though it's as hot here as my imagined Florida. I can hear her catching her breaths roughly, as if they are trying to escape her. The woman in the other bed is gone. There is no need to ask where.

I place the fruit I have brought on the night table, and watch her sleep, wondering how many times she sat like this and watched me through scarlet fever and whooping cough and my screaming night terrors. I wonder if she can sense my presence, as I could sense hers at times, hear her breath and the barely audible slice of a needle through fabric, not opening my eyes. In our busy house, it was enough to half-wake and savour the feeling of having someone look after you, without you having to do or be anything, without having to ingratiate yourself to get love. Daytime she was too harassed, too busy and angry and on edge to show feelings for anyone, but at night she crept into our rooms and occupied our dreams, offering love as silence. It is how I try to occupy her now, although I know that each moment of peace I give her only leans her closer to death.

Death. As it gets dark, I can't stay here; I get jumpy, have to leave. The dark seems deeper here, something that could sweep you away. I feel myself pulled toward sleep. In winter, with the screen of trees and the snow muffling the traffic, you could forget you're alive here. Death is strung out like a drift-net, deep and secret and light and floating. Lethal. Indiscriminate. Drift-nets catch whatever floats by.

On Monday, the phone doesn't ring at all, and I think ahead, prepare myself, for the slim brown envelope frozen to the mailbox. Tomorrow or the next day. Two of them had interviewed me, Lacey, the old man fluttering his hands over papers, and the young one, Cassell, showing off his skills under the old man's watchful eye. Cassell asked me to "elaborate" on the gaps in my resume. Gaps. Cassell, you are only a little older than my oldest son Mike, so what do you know about gaps? What do you know about gaps, or about Mike, another absence in my mailbox I've been worrying about, have trouble getting used to even now. Flesh of my flesh. Gaps.

When I left school, I was only three months from the end of grade eleven. Yet afterwards, although I had spent eleven years in that cold, three-room school, what I had become was a dropout. I had not received the blessed sacrament of the public exams. But in the early seventies, there was no question of staying in school once anyone knew you were pregnant. And of course there was Martin, hovering outside the school, leaning on the fence. We could look out the classroom window and see him there combing his hair. Filling up the window until I had to leave, first school, then the province, for Ontario, land of our dreams.

One day, three years later, after a particularly bad night when he had held me to him by the hair—not pulled, just held—while Mike cried for me in the next room, I wrote him a letter addressed "Dear Caveman" and went to the airport with my son and my roll of hoarded bills and was amazed at how many of them it took to buy two one-way tickets home.

All this washes over me during my long baths; the anger aroused by my young interviewer has brought Mike to mind again, fresh, my frustration kindling. "I don't know the truth about my dad. Only what you tell me," he said one night. He was sixteen and had the yeasty smell of old beer on his breath. He left for Ontario to find Martin. "A fellow needs a job, money, not this friggin school," he said. I knew he was convinced he would form some deep bond with Martin, who must surely love him even if he had refused to support him. Now I construct the details of his life from infrequent letters full of bad spelling and a sense of obligation. He goes drinking with Martin. I imagine them both weeping over pint mugs on Friday nights. Two mama's boys, really, god help them.

The bath is my journal and therapist. I write chains of events in steam, tell my worries to the cracked tiles, imagine everything washing away. The water becomes a stream, a sea. Eyes closed, I dream I am at a spa somewhere, white towels as soft as summer rain. A young masseur pummels the knots out of my back. I walk out a new woman. The stuff of women's magazines, sacraments for the godless.

After the bath, I make tea and lounge on the sofa in a kind of stupor. The phone rings. It is Mrs. Byrd from Greene, White, Hardy and Black, a legal firm that has had my resume for a month. Could I come for an interview on Wednesday or Thursday, and what time would be convenient?

"Oh," I say, hunting around for words. I had assumed the position was filled.

"Sorry for the delay in getting back to you. It's been really busy here. I decided to stay on until things cleared up. But we're ready to interview now. Are you still interested?"

"Oh, yes, of course."

"When would you like to come?"

"Oh, when is it convenient for you—I mean, when would be a good time?"

"We're just setting our schedule now."

"I'll take the last slot, then." Courage, recalling those job-search classes, the first and the last slots are always the best.

"That will be Thursday at 2:00 then. Third floor. See you on Thursday."

Oh, oh, oh, I think when I hang up—why did I keep saying *oh*.

Between Tuesday and Thursday I regret a thousand times my choice of the last slot. Why didn't I pick the first? They will already have made their choice, they will be bored, they will compare me with all the bright young things who have come before. They will do the interview only as a courtesy, already tired of this process, desperate to get on with the real business of their lives. Greene, White, Hardy and Black—Melanie and Joey and I have a real laugh over that one. How did Hardy break through without a name change? I do my research and learn that

Hardy is a woman, she is married to Greene, and has not changed her name. Nothing terrifies me as much as a woman who is on what my job-search mentors used to call a solid career-track.

Wednesday night Joey wakes up hot and hoarse and thirsty. He calls me and cries, "water," as if he's been trekking in the desert and his camel died yesterday. This is serious. Tonsils, again. On Thursday, I call the school, and sit with him as he lies feverish on the sofa, thinking that I should be taking him to the hospital instead of going to a job interview. But outside the wind howls, and snow-devils leap and plunge around the house, and I don't want them attacking his sore throat, and besides I must go.

"I got to go to school tomorrow," he whines. "I got to."

"Why?"

"Cause if I don't I can't have the sleepover. I can't be out sick and have a sleepover . . ."

Oh, yes. I remember now from school—if you're sick in the day, somehow you have to be sick at night too, even if you feel better. In night school, and later at university, it was a revelation to me that students were so casual about sickness. I always worried about the teachers catching me, even when I was in my thirties.

"Tell you what. We'll see the doctor in the morning. I'll get a note. Then you can go tomorrow afternoon, and everything will be all right."

"Mom . . ." he says, looking at me as if I've uttered some near-criminal brilliance.

"Okay? But I have to go out this afternoon. I've got a job interview. Barb'll be in and out from next door to check on you."

I sort the mail while Joey's chicken soup cools. Somehow, tasting for the right temperature, I have slopped the soup, and right where I could wear a tasteful little pin on my shawl collar, a stray noodle curls in a soupy trail on my *creme de faux soie* blouse. Here is Boyd's child support cheque, consistent if consistently late, and frozen to it, a brown envelope containing a letter of rejection which I will later read and file in the bulging brown folder in case UI ever checks up.

I have fantasies about being called up, told to report. I bring the folder down and drop it dramatically on the UI snoop's desk. "See," I say, "Here's the evidence. I *have* been looking. I've done everything right. There just aren't any jobs." I straighten, glare a little. The UI snoop is so impressed with my efforts I'm offered a job on the spot. It pays forty thousand a year.

I lay Boyd's cheque next to the electrical bill, knowing that those two pieces of paper will have a close relationship. Underneath, a lime green and pink envelope shouts in large type YES, YOU, MRS. LAURA BISHOP, YOU MAY BE OUR NEXT MILLIONAIRE. The only other clean blouse that matches my suit is a grey one. The collar is too high, and even when I keep my neck rigid, it pushes a fold of flesh above, an extra little chin. Goddamn Cheryl, she said it looked nice when I tried it on.

Caroline Byrd is a bit of a shock to me. She sort of lounges, parts of her all over her big chair. Her loose auburn hair is streaked with grey. She is wearing a bulky sweater over a long denim skirt and dark tights, flat shoes. No makeup. Not what I'd expected. Now I feel like an overdone over-age doll, with my lipstick and horrible grey blouse, suit and pumps. The red knees protrude through sheer pantyhose, sheer misery. "You must be freezing," she says. On her desk, open, face-down is a copy of Naomi Wolf's *The Beauty Myth*. She places a coffee cup in my hand. "Now," she says, "I might as well be useful and tell you about the position while you wait. It'll keep you from getting nerves.

Not that they're a very threatening bunch, that crowd," she inclines her head toward the closed door.

By the time Patricia Hardy emerges with the previous applicant, a young woman with so much hair she only needs a guitar to embark on a country and western career, I know that Caroline Byrd is about to retire after twenty years. Her husband has been bugging her to spend winters in Florida. My gut constricts in pain when she tells me this; she isn't much older than me. It's a one-woman office she says, they basically want you to run it, do everything except lawyering, keep the operation shipshape. They pay well to rely on you. They don't try to run your life or compete for your attention. There's no dress code, she says, glancing at me. It's an old firm, your job is to project professionalism, competence, confidence.

Those three words are on my lips in soundless repetition when Patricia Hardy shakes my hand, her eyes catching the movement of my lips, perhaps wondering if I'm praying.

The interview went so well I'm smiling as I chop carrots, aware that at 4:15, the office hasn't closed yet, and there may be a decision yet today. I am allowing myself to indulge in hope, a sinful indulgence. Hope, like pride, I have been told most of my life, cometh before a fall.

"Mom, you're going to get that job, and you're going to marry a lawyer!" Melanie teases, waltzing around me. "We'll shop till we drop! We'll move to a big new house in Manderley Estates!"

"Melanie, that's not what it's about, honey. I'm not going to marry a lawyer; I just applied for a job at a legal firm. Besides, I would never live in some housing cul de sac way to hell out there. I like to walk places."

"You wouldn't have to walk. You could get a car. Did Dad's cheque come?"

"Yeah. It's over there getting intimate with the light bill. Now, those two are going to get married."

"What, nothing left?"

"Not much. Why?"

"January sales, Mom. I need jeans."

"You have jeans."

"I don't have new jeans."

"I thought they were supposed to look old."

"Look old, not be old."

"I'll see," I tell her, "I'll see." I'll see. I'll see.

By six, I know the office has closed. No chance that Caroline Byrd and Patricia Hardy are down on Duckworth Street in a snowstorm discussing my brilliant qualifications. I doctor Joey's fever, then hold him close on the sofa while we watch TV, until he complains my arm is too tight and I'm making him sweat.

The last job I had was with a feminist production company planning to do a film about women's issues during the great propaganda racket that concluded with Newfoundland's Confederation with Canada in 1949. It was one of those fiftieth anniversary of Confederation projects. It was the first job like that I'd ever had—exciting, working as part of a team, delving like a detective in the Provincial Archives. It was one of those government grants where you get to do interesting work for a pretty bad salary. You're called a trainee, and you're supposed to learn new skills that will make you more marketable. I still find it funny. Employers must be beating the woods looking for someone who knows about women and Confederation propaganda. It looks weird on my resume now, but I enjoyed it, the work and wearing jeans and always going out to lunch. The talk, most of all. I still keep a quote from my research on the fridge, next to the bills. It's from the May, 1948 edition of *The Confeder-ate*, Joey Smallwood's pro-Canadian propaganda tool. It says:

> Mothers, Read This
>> EVERY MOTHER in Newfoundland should vote for Confederation.
>> Never mind what the **politicians** say. Never mind what the **newspapers** say. Never mind what the **men** say.
>> If you have children YOU SHOULD VOTE FOR THEM.
>> Once we get Confederation we know that NEVER AGAIN WILL THERE BE A HUNGRY CHILD IN NEWFOUNDLAND.

And it was during that job that I began to imagine my mother. Floating above the pages of archaic propaganda and cheap shots, I could see her walking from Nan's house to Cuthbert's Shop to our house, her short boots and woollen stockings no match for the deep snows of Hampton's Harbour during the spring of 1948. She would have felt the first stirrings of my sister inside her then, growing vigorous and strong, becoming a large baby despite the poor times, the fifth of seven children that would conclude with me. I wondered as the winter broke how much of the propaganda had reached her, if the smiling sellers of contradictory paradises had come and drove their cars through the bog up to the premises of Nathan Cuthbert, Merchant, and if they had drunk rum there and then spoke standing on boxes on the corner to be taller than everyone else. And then I got the idea that I would interview her, find out to what degree my sister, born in the late fall of 1948, was really Confederation's daughter.

I didn't get her to say much. It was one of her good days, and it was pleasurable to be able to take work time and spend it with her. As if she mattered in the greater scheme of things. But she said she had forgotten everything, it was so long ago, until I asked her how she'd voted.

"I voted for the baby bonus." she said.

I held my silence.

"My dear," she said, after a long time, "I never cared what men ran the country. So far as I was concerned they're all alike. Or even what the country was called, or what flag it flew. I voted for the baby bonus."

She picked at her afghan, "But your . . . dad . . ." Her mind drifted.

I caught her eye to bring her mind back. "Dad . . . what?"

"Oh, he didn't like it, not one bit. He said I was one of the ones selling our country. He said, what did I think, that he couldn't look after us."

I went back to work that afternoon thinking of my mother voting for the baby bonus, voting for her children just like Smallwood wanted, risking my father's considerable anger. And then I got sentimental because, after all, none of us could look after her now. Not any of the six still living. And I got sad because she'd been to my place and knew how I lived.

The green light on the answering machine is blinking when I get back at 1:00 from the doctor and Joey's school. I run and fumble, try to turn it on with my mittens, can't, then pull them off, throw mittens and clattering keys to the floor. Caroline Byrd's smooth voice is like a silk scarf floating out into the still apartment air. "Laura, congratulations, the job is yours if you want it. You'll have to come in, of course, and discuss training period arrangements, salary, benefits and the like. Please call as soon as you get home."

My eyes are full of tears. It's permanent, I keep repeating, it's a permanent job. It doesn't matter if the salary isn't too great. I hear myself saying to someone at the bank, "Yes, my job is permanent. Unless the world suddenly decides it doesn't need any lawyers, ha-ha." The man in the chalk-stripes laughs with me, "Highly unlikely, isn't it, ha-ha. Laura," he says, looking me deep in the eyes and telling me the one thing I've always wanted to hear from a man, "You're a good credit risk."

On Saturday night, Cheryl and I go to Krista's Place, a new hot spot that Cheryl is fond of. But I draw the line at sofas. "No way, Cheryl. I could stay home and sit on a sofa and drink beer. I want you across a table from me, elbows on the glass, hanging onto my every word."

Cheryl laughs, tossing her hair around because the room is full of men dragging out happy hour.

"Melanie didn't mind staying home with Joey?"

"Melanie didn't have a choice. I said, 'You want new-old jeans, you stay home tonight.' Now that I'm working, my boss value has shot up."

"Oh, Laura, a permanent job—you're going to be such a tyrant."

"I'm scared of me too, Cheryl." I say with a straight face, and we both collapse in laughter.

"So who will I go shopping with now?"

"Oh, Cheryl, people with jobs shop. They must. They must shop more than us."

"But it won't be the same. Are you sure this is what you want to do, I mean back at secretarial work again? And does it really pay enough?"

"Oh, the pay is fine. And," I say, pulling a Caroline Byrd, "it's not secretarial work—I'll be running the office."

"See those guys, over there."

I look and see two men slouching in identical trench coats.

One of them keeps touching his bare scalp tentatively, as if expecting to feel the fine sprouts of new hair.

"They're giving us the eye. If they come over, you can practice on them. Tell them you're an office manager. If they ask who you've got under you, say, 'Only the boss.' "

"Jesus, Cheryl. Is that another Gerald-joke?"

"Gerald is kind of weird in bed, I got to say." Cheryl tells me this before running to the bar for more drinks to help her tell her story. At the bar, a man with poet-eyes engages her in conversation, then uses the opportunity to bum one of her cigarettes.

I sit back to watch this little episode, linking my fingers behind my neck, stretching, opening my body in a way I rarely do. The room is full of men, but they all seem old, even though most of them are probably around my age. I don't feel very old this evening.

A woman my age is in her prime, so say the glossy magazines I'm ashamed to buy but can't resist at Afterwords. I have read that when a woman moves beyond bearing children and caring for infants, when she has lived through relationships and work experiences, she emerges with a kind of irresistible wisdom, a freedom that makes her both desirous and desirable. I wonder if such power can apply to a woman who has just got her first permanent job at the age of forty-four.

Maybe. But it doesn't seem to matter. Since yesterday, all I've felt is relief, and a pain that's been occupying the centre of my back has moved up, ready to exit through my shoulders. With any luck, it won't continue upward and blow the top off my head, just when things seem to be going well.

I am dreaming of small things while I watch Cheryl and wait for her to return and tell me stories. A fat novel, never opened, lying on the night table. A thick, white terry robe pulled from a clothesline and wrapped around the body after a bath scented with magnolia. A slow lonely lunch in a restaurant with winter melting outside, stir-fry with cashews on a bed of rice. Morning in August somewhere, coffee on the deck of a rented cabin, Joey breathing softly in the next room. Through the trees a lake shines in the sunlight.

Acknowledgements

Thanks to the Canada Council for the Arts, the Newfoundland and Labrador Arts Council and the City of St. John's Arts Jury for support during the period in which these stories were written.

Thanks to the Killick Press editorial board, especially Anne Hart, for useful suggestions on the manuscript.

As always, a great thanks is owed to the community of writers whose support, friendship and critical feedback I value greatly.

And much thanks is owed to my family—to my brothers and sisters for ongoing support, to Ken and Leah for being there when the work is done.

Some of these stories have appeared, sometimes in different form, in: *TickleAce*, *The New Quarterly*, *Event*, *The Antigonish Review* and *The Journey Prize Anthology*.